'I'm paying court to you!' Guy announced sardonically.

Jane was sure her face must be blood-red, and it wasn't even as if it were the truth . . .

'That's a very strange thing to say,' she muttered stiffly. 'People don't say things like that these days.'

'It's an explicit and accurate term. I like it.'

'Yes . . . but it isn't true.'

'Why shouldn't it be?'

'Because you're making no attempt to be nice to me!'

Dear Reader

Summer might be drawing to an end—but don't despair! This month's selection of exciting love stories is guaranteed to bring back a little sunshine! Why not let yourself be transported to the beauty of a Caribbean paradise—or perhaps you'd prefer the exotic mystery of Egypt? All in the company of a charming and devastatingly handsome hero, naturally! Of course, you don't have to go abroad to find true romance—and when you're a Mills & Boon reader you don't even need to step outside your front door! Just relax with this book, and you'll see what we mean . . .

The Editor

Jenny Cartwright was born and raised in Wales. After three years at university in Kent and a year spent in America, she returned to Wales where she has lived and worked ever since. Happily married with three young children—a girl and two boys—she began to indulge her lifelong desire to write when her lively twins were very small. The peaceful solitude she enjoys while creating her romances contrasts happily with the often hectic bustle of her family life.

Recent titles by the same author:

BITTER POSSESSION
BLAMELESS DESIRE
PASSIONATE OPPONENT

FORSAKING ALL REASON

BY
JENNY CARTWRIGHT

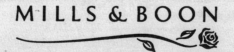

MILLS & BOON

MILLS & BOON LIMITED
ETON HOUSE, 18-24 PARADISE ROAD
RICHMOND, SURREY TW9 1SR

*MILLS & BOON and the Rose Device
are trademarks of the publisher.*

*First published in Great Britain 1994
by Mills & Boon Limited*

© Jenny Cartwright 1994

*Australian copyright 1994   Philippine copyright 1994
This edition 1994*

ISBN 0 263 78624 2

*Set in Times Roman 10 on 11¼ pt.
01-9409-56749 C*

Made and printed in Great Britain

CHAPTER ONE

IT WAS obvious that it hadn't worked. For a start, the moment Jane arrived at the top of the wide, curving staircase she found herself blinking madly, as if she'd just emerged from the cinema on a sunny afternoon. The big square hallway beneath was as brilliantly lit as an operating theatre, and just about as enticing. She stood mournfully on the top stair, her hand resting lightly on the mahogany banister rail, and sighed.

With an unfamiliar click of high heels her mother appeared in the space below. 'Ready, darling?' she called, smiling up at her daughter.

'Yes. I'm on my way down now, Mum,' Jane replied brightly.

'What do you think?' her mother returned uncertainly. 'Do you think it's done the trick?'

Jane fingered the small sapphire stud on one earlobe and turned it slowly before replying. 'Er...well, it's a bit difficult to judge from up here...'

'But it does look brighter, doesn't it?'

'Oh, yes, Mum,' said Jane comfortingly, twisting the earring a little faster. 'It certainly looks much...brighter.'

She started to descend the shallow, curved steps, her pretty feet in their navy and silver sandals carefully judging distances on the burgundy carpet, while her eyes remained transfixed by the scene below. Perhaps it would look different once she got lower down. Perhaps the new high-wattage light bulbs, which her mother had specially ordered, and which had taken them all morning to install, would create a much kinder effect at ground level.

5

Perhaps it would look cheerful and welcoming and airy, just as Mum had intended.

It didn't. It looked harsh and cold, the stone-flagged floor scoured by the cruel white light.

'It was so very *gloomy* before...' her mother continued with a frown, looking about her.

'It was,' agreed Jane, nodding seriously.

And then her mother's bright blue eyes met Jane's dark brown ones and they both stared at one another for a moment before bursting into gales of laughter.

'Oh, well,' shrugged Wendy Garston at last, 'it was worth a try. And anyway, no one will be looking at the house. They'll only have eyes for you, darling. You look absolutely stunning.'

Jane spun around, pleased by her mother's approval. Her dress, which clung to her slight, neat-waisted form, swirled from the hips where the midnight-blue silk— pricked here and there by a silver thread—flared out into an amazing fullness as it was captured by the whirlwind of air.

'You don't think Daddy will disapprove?' she asked worriedly, coming to a breathless halt and tucking in her chin to look down at the neckline.

'Oh, probably... But don't worry. He ought to be jolly glad that you've got such a nice cleavage to distract the guests.'

Jane pulled a rueful face. 'Everybody's been here hundreds of times. I can't imagine they'll give a hoot about the light bulbs—or my appearance, come to that.'

'They *haven't* all been before,' murmured her mother vaguely. 'There's that chap Daddy and I had dinner with at the country club last week. He's coming...and I rather think your father wants to impress him. We'll have to sit him next to your bosom and see if that does the trick.'

Jane smiled broadly, her eyes twinkling. 'If he gets his sunglasses out, I shall take lots of deep breaths,' she announced, giving a demonstration, then added teasingly, 'It's a good job I put my hair up tonight. It won't spoil the view!' and she patted her glossy, black hair, which was twisted into a stylish topknot.

They were sitting in the floodlit drawing-room, sipping sherries, when the doorbell rang for the first time. They sighed, and exchanged wry glances before standing up and smoothing down their dresses. It was going to be a deadly evening, and they both knew it. Jane's mother loathed giving parties. The trouble was that having lived all her life in the same house she was still considered a bright young thing by the now ageing friends of her late parents—and had too strong a sense of loyalty to leave them off the guest list. In fact, the parties these days were thrown almost entirely for their sakes—if only they knew it. Wendy Garston herself would much prefer to be spending her evening sitting quietly in front of the fire with a good seed catalogue.

By contrast, Jane, at twenty-one, usually looked forward to parties. As long as they weren't her parents' parties, that was. She crossed the room to take her father's arm as he hurried in to join them.

'Langfords have arrived,' he huffed. 'Early as usual. One of those little girls in black from the agency is doing the honours—she'll show them through in a minute, no doubt...' and he ran a finger around his starched collar. Then his eyes dropped to take in Jane's neckline. 'Don't you think that's a bit——?'

'Daddy! What do you think of the lighting?' interrupted his daughter, mischievously catching her mother's eye.

'Lighting?' he asked, obviously baffled. 'Where?'

He was still blinking his bewildered grey eyes when the long, thin, middle-aged Langfords appeared. They were soon followed by the short, stout MacMillans and then Sir Richard with his elderly mother and Colonel

Fish. Anthea Legate with her diminutive husband, Stefanie and Brad Hogg, and the alarmingly intellectual Rene Britten soon followed. By nine o'clock the drawing-room and hall were filled with enough people to soak up any amount of excess light—except that they didn't. The unforgiving luminescence made the men look ill and the women garish. Everyone's nose cast a dark shadow. Only Jane, with her honey-gold skin and blue-black hair, managed to look as if she was bathed in sunshine.

By ten o'clock Jane had switched to mineral water. She had been around the cold buffet twice and was wishing that the caterers would hurry up and produce the profiteroles which she had spied earlier in the kitchen. Like her mother, she was a dutiful and enthusiastic hostess, but despite their joint efforts the evening was proving as boring as they had both known it would be. She leant her bare shoulders against a vacant bit of wall and closed her eyes. When she felt a warm, dry hand lay itself on her arm she thought it must be her father.

She didn't bother to open her eyes. 'Hi...' she said warmly. 'Just taking a breather...'

'Good,' returned a deep male voice. 'I thought you might be feeling unwell.'

Jane lazily opened her large, almond-shaped eyes very wide. 'Oh, dear...' she said, feeling a smile dimpling her cheeks. That most certainly hadn't been her father's voice!

However, when she looked beyond the starched and pleated shirt-front, up past the clean square jawline, to the slaty, blue-black eyes which were looking down on her from a great height, the desire to smile disappeared altogether.

The man's own mouth, though naturally well-shaped, made a straight, unyielding line across the hard planes of his face. His dark brown hair was cut very short, his skin was tanned, and his eyebrows, which were smooth and straight and very, very black, gave as little away as the severe line of his mouth. It was a very masculine face. And for some unaccountable reason Jane had the feeling that, despite its well-governed expression, the face was disapproving of her.

'How do you do?' she said politely, making her own mouth remember its manners and smile again. 'I'm fine, as it happens. Just a little tired, thank you all the same.'

The man's hand still lay lightly on her upper arm. She had to fight the urge to turn her head to look at it. It might seem as if she was suggesting it had no right to be there, when in fact she was the ill-mannered one, closing her eyes on the guests. There would have been no need for him to have touched her if she'd been behaving as she ought.

'How do you do?' returned the dark, gravelly voice, perfectly correctly. 'You certainly don't look ill, now that you've opened your eyes.'

'Unlike...' She stopped herself. She had been going to say humorously, Unlike all the men here tonight. But the fact was that this man, with his taut, bronzed skin, didn't look the least bit pale. His straight nose cast no shadow. Instead, the light on his face enhanced the clean sweep of his brow and gave prominence to his cheekbones, lending no more than a faint umbra to the hollows of his cheeks, and emphasising the hard angularity of his countenance. He was extremely good-looking, she decided privately.

'So you find parties tiring, do you?' enquired the man.

'Er...not all parties. But this one *has* been rather hard work, I have to admit.'

'The food's very good. Worth the effort.'

'Oh. I didn't mean that. Actually the food's all been done by caterers.' It was her mother's one indulgence.

'Then what did you mean?'

'Oh ... you know. I'm the daughter of the house, so I've been been doing all the introductions and socialising and that sort of thing.'

'And you consider *that* hard work?'

Jane opened her mouth to reply. But before she could get the words out he said drily, 'Don't bother to explain. I started working for real when I was just eight years old. I'm afraid you and I are likely to have very different ideas on the meaning of the word.'

Jane gave a tight smile. She felt well and truly put in her place. 'Well,' she said briskly after a moment's pause, 'to get back to work—*my* kind of work, that is—let me introduce myself. I'm——'

'Jane Garston. I know,' he said matter-of-factly. One eyebrow had flickered slightly, warning her of his intention to interrupt. It was the first time his features had betrayed anything at all. 'I'm Guy Rexford. I dined with your parents last week.'

'Uh-huh ... I remember them mentioning it.' So *this* was the man Jane was supposed to be impressing ... ?

Unthinkingly, she lowered her dark eyes and surveyed the swooping neckline of her dress. The lights were casting the deepest, darkest shadow imaginable between her high, rounded breasts. Oh, drat! She wished now that she and her mother hadn't make that silly joke. She didn't much like the idea of distracting Guy Rexford with her cleavage. He was much too young—well, compared to the other guests, anyway—and much too austere to be the butt of such humour. She wouldn't even have worn the dress had she not thought the entire company would consist of respectable old fogeys. She hunched her shoulders slightly and tried her hardest not to breathe deeply.

'What are you looking at?' asked Guy Rexford levelly. There was something about his dark, well-modulated voice which was disconcerting. It was, so far at any rate, as well-controlled as his features, and yet there were nuances and depths to its timbre which disconcerted her.

Jane looked up guiltily. She hadn't realised her inspection was so obvious. The warmth of her embarrassment began to soak into her skin, but luckily, given her colouring, her blushes rarely showed.

'Nothing,' she said sheepishly.

'You were,' he contradicted.

'I...um...I dropped a peanut earlier...' she said hastily, and then the warmth intensified as she realised that she had only made matters worse. 'It's all right, though. I—er—I think it went on the floor. I expect somebody's trodden on it by now,' she continued balefully.

She looked up into his eyes, expecting to find... lechery? Scorn? Instead she found them as enigmatically neutral as before.

'Then you won't want me to try to find it for you?'

'No, thank you,' she muttered falteringly.

He let his hand fall away from her arm almost disdainfully. 'Are you sure that doesn't mean "yes, please"?'

Now she understood just what it was that his voice had intimated moments before. He spoke so caustically that she felt grazed by his words. His voice was a tool. A sharp-edged tool. She felt as if he had just drawn it menacingly across her throat. And yet his features still gave nothing away.

Jane swallowed, then bit hard on the inside of her tilted upper lip. 'I didn't mean...' She clenched her fists defensively. What on earth could she say? The man seemed to be suggesting that she positively wanted him to look down the front of her dress... 'No, of course it doesn't! What an absurd idea—trying to find a lost *peanut*.'

'Well, that's all right, then,' he said laconically.

'Is it?' she returned, fierily. 'I don't happen to think it's all right at all. I'm not used to having men talk to me like that, *Mr* Rexford.'

'Like what?' he countered wryly. 'Don't the gentlemen of your acquaintance usually offer to help you, *Miss* Garston?'

'The gentlemen of my acquaintance...' she began haughtily, and then began to flounder. 'Well, they *are* gentlemen. That's all.'

'And I'm not?'

'I didn't say that,' she muttered guardedly. This was awful. She seemed to have started an argument—and yet she had no idea what the argument was about. Except for a mythical lost peanut, of course... 'I'm sorry,' she sighed, looking up at him for a clue as to how to set things right. But his features were unreadable again, unreadable but not forgiving. Suddenly she wanted to walk away from him very fast, her chin high.

But he beat her to it. 'It's been nice meeting you, Jane Garston...' he drawled, turning to go. His dark blue eyes swept scathingly over her bare shoulders, before very obviously, and not the least bit salaciously, studying the shadow between her breasts.

'Er...goodbye...' she said.

He made his way swiftly through the gaggle of guests. Annoyingly, she found her eyes following him. He was several inches over six feet, much taller than the rest of the company, and he remained perfectly visible until he reached the front door. He turned a little as he twisted the heavy iron ring on the solid-oak door. To one side of his face, just below his left cheekbone, was a dark mole. It lent that particular aspect of his face a surprising beauty. But when the door came open he tilted his head the other way and the vision fled. The man who closed the door behind him was big, powerfully built, with such an uncompromisingly granite cast to his features that he could never, ever be described as *beautiful*.

Jane remained leaning against the wall for a few moments, waiting for her skin to cool down. Then she hailed Colonel Fish as he staggered by, biting a squidgy profiterole. She allowed him to bore her rigid for the rest of the evening. There was a lot to be said for being bored, after all.

When the last guest had gone, Wendy and Sidney Garston occupied their usual chairs on either side of the fireplace. Both had eased off their shoes, and looked tired.

'Come to say goodnight, sweetheart?' asked her father, as Jane brought her cocoa through to join them.

'Yes. I'll drink this in bed. I'm worn out. It went very well, though, didn't it?'

Her father pulled a face. 'It took a nosedive just before ten. I thought that Rexford chap wasn't going to turn up until then.'

'Didn't you want him to come?'

Sidney Garston ran a blue-veined hand through his thinning fair hair. 'Not really, love. I was hoping he'd lost interest in me. I've got a nasty feeling he's planning to take over Garston's, you see. He tried to poach a couple of my top design engineers a couple of weeks ago, and then when we went out for that meal with Molly and Leonard it turned out he'd wangled an invite. He spent the whole evening asking about the firm—though why he bothered I can't imagine. He already knew as much about it as I do.'

'But that doesn't mean he's going to take you over, Dad, surely? Anyway, Garston's is a private company, and there are still plenty of shares in family hands. I thought that made you safe?'

Sidney Garston shrugged. 'So did I. But it's not actually impossible for someone to take us over. Only improbable.'

Her mother sighed. 'If only Aunt Florrie hadn't left all those shares to that wretched cats' home... I suppose we can't blame her, because the poor soul was quite batty, but it has meant that something like this has been a possibility for years now.' She nibbled her lip. 'We should have tried to get hold of those shares, Sidney.'

Her father shrugged dispiritedly. 'I've always invested whatever capital I have in the business, love. It's one of the reasons I've managed to keep it buoyant through all these recessions. If I'd used our money to increase our holding we wouldn't have been able to invest in all those computerised lathes for a start, and we might well have gone under. It's never felt like much of an option.'

'But why would Guy Rexford want to buy Garston's, Dad?' intruded Jane with a worried frown. She had never seen her father like this before, and it hurt her to see his usually cheerful face looking vulnerable and exposed.

'Guy Rexford does exactly as he pleases in the world of engineering,' said her father greyly. 'Rexford Holdings has swallowed up much bigger firms than ours in recent years. I think he's probably after my research and development team.' He sighed leadenly. 'And what Rexford wants he gets. Or that's the story everybody tells.'

'Oh,' said Jane, looking sympathetically at her father. From what little she'd seen of Guy Rexford, she could well believe it was true. 'So he could just...just throw you out? After everything you've done for the firm? Daddy, it's been in your family for generations! You live and breathe that smelly factory!'

Her father gave one of his deep, rumbling chuckles. 'It's not that drastic, Jane, my love. I doubt he'll throw me on the scrap-heap. He'll just tie my hands a bit. Never fear, I shall still spend the greater part of my life in that smelly factory, as you so charmingly call it. And if he does force me out he'll make a very wealthy man of me in the process.'

'But you'd *hate* sitting at home being rich!' wailed Jane.

Wendy Garston smiled comfortingly at her husband. 'Now be fair, Sidney. You don't know that he'll do anything at all. It's only speculation...'

'It was until this evening, my love. When I invited him to come along I was testing the water. If he hadn't had any designs on us he wouldn't have turned up at all. Instead of which, he marches in here as late as you please, stays five minutes and then swans off. It speaks for itself.'

'So his coming here tonight was symbolic?' asked Jane, praying that her own unfortunate encounter with him wouldn't affect anything. Then she set down her cocoa and went across to hug her father. 'Never mind, Daddy, darling. Even if he ruins *your* life, Mummy and I will do everything *we* can, every minute of the day, to let you know how happy we are to be terribly, disgustingly rich. Won't we, Mum?'

It was just the right thing to have said. Her parents' faces broke into broad smiles, and the mood of gloom evaporated, leaving the little family relaxed and at ease to pick over the bones of the other guests.

Two mornings in a row spent on the top of a rickety step-ladder changing light bulbs was about as much as Jane could bear. Especially as she'd had to retrieve the old ones from the bin, wearing rubber gloves, and had then had to wash them and make sure they were bone-dry before connecting them to the electricity supply.

She saved the hall till last, mainly because it was so forbiddingly dark without any light at all. In fact she'd had to prop the front door wide open in order to be able to see what she was doing. A gusty breeze charged in and rattled the steps.

'Still looking for that peanut?' came a voice that already she would know anywhere.

She ducked her head out from the centre of the huge chandelier, and shook her shoulder-length hair back from her face. What on earth was *he* doing here? 'I'm changing the light bulbs,' she said a little obviously, holding out one of the candle-flame-shaped bulbs for inspection.

It should have given her an advantage, looking down on him. But of course it didn't. He was leaning against the door, his hands in the pockets of his suit jacket, and one foot crossed over the other at the ankle.

'You do surprise me . . .' There was a dry bluntness in his voice right now which almost bordered on the humorous. She eyed him suspiciously.

'Didn't you notice how strong the lighting was last night?' she asked lamely, tucking the bulb in her jeans pocket and then taking it out again. 'We got the wattage wrong.'

'Indeed.'

'So . . . um . . . Look, if you want my father, I'm afraid he's not home. He's at work.'

'I don't want your father.'

'Oh. Mother's around somewhere. In the kitchen, I think.' She put the bulb back in the box on top of the steps, wiped her hands on her jeans, then began to come down the ladder.

But before she had taken more than a couple of steps he had crossed the flagged floor and caught hold of her at the waist, swinging her down on to the floor beside him.

He left his hands in place. 'I don't want to see your mother.'

Flustered, she pushed his hands away. Very slowly and very deliberately he put them back.

It was a horrible feeling having Guy Rexford's big square hands sitting lightly on the curve of her waist. She was wearing a huge, fuchsia sweatshirt with her T-shirt and jeans, but despite the layers of clothing she was more than conscious of the weight of his hands on her flesh. And the awful thing was that the feeling was exciting. Very exciting. It tied a tangled knot in her stomach and made her feel as if breathing was an art she had only recently learned. And yet *this* was the man who was about to ruin everything her father lived for. She felt sick with herself.

'Please take your hands off me,' she said shakily.

He did. He lifted his splayed hands away from her waist and let them drop to his sides.

'Why did you do that?' she asked furiously.

'Because I wanted to.'

'Oh.' Jane glowered at him from under her thick straight fringe. He looked back at her unflinchingly. It made her feel dreadfully flummoxed.

In their brief verbal exchanges to date she hadn't exactly given a very good account of herself. Peering down at her own bosom had been bad enough, especially as he had made it seem as if she was practically inviting him into her bed. And now, when she needed to say exactly the right thing—the thing which would let him know in no uncertain terms that she wasn't that sort of girl, while at the same time preserving the peace for her father's sake—well, now her mind was a complete blank. And *he* was no help at all. He just stood there, in the only patch of light in the entire hall, and waited for her to speak. All she could think was that his eyes looked greyer in daylight.

She cleared her throat. 'I don't think that's a very good reason for...um...for...' She let out a quivering sigh.

Oh, dear. Supposing she offended him and he bought Garston's out of spite?

'*Molesting* you? But I didn't, Jane Garston. You're jumping the gun. I merely helped you down from the step-ladder.'

'*And* put your hands on my... my middle when I'd already taken them away.'

One of those very black eyebrows moved very slightly upwards. 'I wanted to see if you meant it,' he said. 'Now that I know that you did, I shan't do it again without being invited.' Again that dangerous edge was back in his voice.

'Then you *won't* do it again,' she said decisively, arching her brows. 'Now, how can I help you, Mr Rexford? Did you leave something behind last night?'

He inclined his head gravely to one side. 'Yes. You.'

'Me!'

He allowed a small smile to curve his mouth, but his eyes remained neutral. 'I've come to court you, Jane Garston. I shall begin by taking you out to lunch.'

Jane's heart started to hammer madly, and her mouth became inexplicably dry. What an extraordinary thing to say! And yet it hadn't sounded the least bit odd, coming from him. That voice of his—even when saying the most mundane things—promised such devastation that even a comment like that came almost as an anticlimax.

'Why do you call me Jane Garston?' she said at length, a small frown furrowing her brow. She honestly couldn't think of anything else to say that wouldn't sound completely stupid. She certainly couldn't bring herself to refer to his assertion that he had come to court her.

'It's your name,' he returned levelly. And then he turned and walked briskly to a small door on his left, opened it, and stooped slightly to pass through. Within seconds he had emerged with a burnt-orange anorak in his hands.

'Catch,' he said, and tossed it to her.

'How did you know that was the cloakroom? And how did you know that jacket was mine?'

He shrugged, and smiled enigmatically. 'Now run along and tell your mother you'll be having lunch with me. You'll be back in an hour and a half.'

She ran the ridged edge of the zip between her fingers and then nipped one of the notches hard between her forefinger and thumb. 'I haven't said I'll come,' she said crossly.

'Hurry,' he replied. 'I'm short of time as it is...'

'But——'

'Go on. You don't want to keep me waiting, now do you?'

And to her dismay she found herself turning biddably towards the kitchen to find her mother. What should she do? If she'd met him at one of her friends' parties she'd have been thrilled to be noticed by him. She certainly would have jumped at the chance of a date with him—well, assuming he'd been introduced and everything and she knew something about him, that was. He was so...well, so attractive. And that remote, self-contained manner of his, while decidedly frightening, was undeniably intriguing. But she *hadn't* met him like that. She'd met him because he was interested in the family firm. No doubt his plan was to ply her with drinks and pump her for information. The realisation made Jane giggle softly to herself. He wouldn't get very far on that score! She didn't know anything about engineering.

'Off out, darling?' her mother asked, looking up from her perusal of the newspaper.

'How did you——? Oh, the coat... Sorry. My brain's not working properly.'

'Well, *make* it work if you're planning to drive your car!'

'I'm not. Mum, the thing is, Guy Rexford's just appeared and asked me to have lunch with him.'

Her mother's spectacles had slipped down to the end of her nose. She peered over them. 'Has he? How exciting, darling.'

Jane pulled a face. 'Why did you say that?'

'Well, he's very handsome and very eligible. And you've obviously decided to accept, or you wouldn't have your coat with you, now would you? So run along and have a good time...'

Jane took a deep breath. She wanted to explain to her mother... And yet how could she explain the churning excitement which his fraudulent declaration had stirred in her stomach? It was all too complicated. On the whole, she decided it would be a lot easier just to go with him, and explain things later. After all, he wouldn't ask her again when he realised how useless she was going to be as a mole.

When she got back to the hall it was to find that the light bulbs had all been replaced, and the step-ladder was neatly propped against the wall under the stairs.

'No one will trip over it there,' he said, and offered her his arm in a strangely old-fashioned way. Reluctantly she took it, glad that she now had her anorak as well as the sweatshirt and T-shirt, not to mention his jacket sleeve and shirt, as a barrier between them. She balled her small fist loosely rather than let her hand lie on his sleeve, and walked nervously through the door at his side. He reached back to pull it closed.

'I take it you don't want to leave the door open now the lights are working again?' he said.

Jane screwed up her face. 'You seem to know everything, without ever being told,' she complained.

'I simply keep my eyes and ears open,' he said. 'It's enough.'

Outside the air was damp and fresh. Their feet crunched on the gravel driveway as they made their way to the box-hedge which screened the parking area from the house. Jane found herself wondering where he would take her. 'I'm not very clean,' she said conversationally, and then tore her hand away from his arm to cover her mouth. 'That sounded awful,' she moaned apologetically.

Guy looked down on her, his eyes as enigmatic as ever and his mouth its usual straight line. 'Such things are relative. I don't doubt you showered this morning.'

'Well, yes. Of course. But the thing is—well, what I meant was, I've been up that step-ladder all morning and I'm only wearing jeans and a sweatshirt.'

'I'd noticed. Don't worry. I shan't shame you by taking you somewhere exclusive, Jane Garston.'

'Oh.'

They rounded the hedge and Jane got her first sight of his gleaming black Lotus. It was beautifully streamlined and very, very impressive.

He opened the passenger door. 'Get in,' he said.

She got into the low-slung seat and fumbled with her seatbelt while he came round and swung himself in behind the wheel.

'Direct me to a good pub,' he said as he pulled out of the driveway. 'I don't know the area.'

'Good grief!' she exclaimed impulsively, forgetting her intention not to risk offending him. 'You do surprise me. What's the matter... is there something wrong with those famous eyes of yours? Did you drive here blindfold? I thought *you* of all people would have noticed one on the way here, *and* memorised the menu pinned up outside as you flashed by at a hundred miles an hour!'

And then Guy Rexford did the most surprising thing he had done so far. He smiled broadly, revealing strong even white teeth and then he tipped his head back and laughed richly.

The sound seemed confined by the enclosed car. It seemed to fill the space around her with its deep, resonant notes. It made her skin hug her very tight, and her mouth feel dry and useless again. Because it made him sound human... And that was more frightening than anything.

CHAPTER TWO

IRONICALLY, Guy drove straight into the car park of a country inn without taking any directions at all from her. Admittedly they had to pass it before they got to the main road, and it had a sign outside indicating that hot lunches were available. Even so...

'I wasn't going to suggest this place,' she said obscurely.

He looked down into her eyes, his face uncannily managing to suggest disapproval again, though there was no obvious expression there. 'I know. You thought it might be too ordinary. But I haven't much time to spare today, as I've already mentioned.'

'Oh.' He was right. She *had* dismissed the Three Bells as being too ordinary for a man like him, though she and her mother often had lunch there. 'Well, I did think it might be a bit... you know... not quite your style.'

'What made you think I'd turn up my nose at it, Jane?'

'Well, I don't know. You just give off the aura of someone with impossibly high standards.'

'How clever of you.'

'Ah! So I was right.'

'Not exactly. I do have high standards, it's true. But I always make them suit the purpose. In my view, a good pub lunch is usually simple and unpretentious, and is most likely to be found in a simple and unpretentious pub. Caviare sandwiches right now I do not want.'

'Well, yes, but there's a place with a French chef where they do little——'

23

'If the French chef's doing no more than providing good pub fare then he's either not much of a chef or he's wasting his talents. Don't you agree?'

She sighed heavily, then flapped her hands. 'Look...I...I didn't know a simple meal could turn into an intellectual debate. If I had I certainly wouldn't have come. I'm not the academic type. So if you want to wipe the floor with me, go right ahead. It should prove easy.'

'You're not trying to tell me that you're the doormat type, are you, Jane Garston?'

'Doormats are used for wiping shoes—not floors,' she returned snappily.

He chuckled. 'Ah. I stand corrected. It seems you have just metaphorically wiped the floor with me.'

'Good. I'd feel so much better for that if only I believed it was true. Now can we go in and order? I'm starving.'

'OK. This place looks fine,' he said, getting out.

'Actually, it is quite good,' she confirmed reluctantly, trying not to meet his eye, and struggling to dispel her irritation. Why should she be so convinced that he despised her? What reason had she given him, after all?

She let her gaze settle about shoulder level. His suit was black with a blue pinstripe, and was superbly well-cut. It was soberly single-breasted. He wore it without a waistcoat, revealing an expanse of fine white linen shirt on either side of his narrow, dark tie. Actually, the tie was unusually narrow. It wasn't that it didn't look good—it did. But it certainly wasn't the obvious tie to wear with a business suit. She found it unnerving, just that tiny sartorial break with convention seemed to be enough to suggest that he was a man who would break any rule he chose.

'Come on, Jane Garston,' he said crisply. 'Lead the way. You know which is the best bar.'

'I'm honoured,' she returned, relieved to feel her usual good humour beginning to seep back at this apparent vote of confidence. She pushed open the door to the lounge where a fire burned brightly.

Once in, however, he took charge, leading the way to the table nearest the window, and flagging a barmaid to come and clear it for them. The service was instantly forthcoming.

Pushing his chair back from the table he stretched out his long legs. 'I'll have trout,' he said decisively, closing the menu and dismissing the barmaid.

'So will I,' rejoined Jane.

He smiled. 'So I was right. The trout is good here?'

'Now how can you possibly know that?' she returned challengingly.

He shrugged his broad shoulders carelessly. 'The lady next to the door is eating it. It looks good. And you've eaten here before, and you've ordered it, so I presume it must taste good too.'

Jane put her elbows on the table and rested her chin in her hands. 'If you don't mind my saying so, Mr Rexford, this business of your knowing everything without being told is getting a little wearing. And I doubt I've spent as much as twenty minutes in your presence so far. If you keep it up for the whole hour and a half I think I shall scream.' She pursed her lips.

'You can call me Guy,' he said levelly.

'You didn't respond to what I said.'

'Isn't the fish good here?'

'Yes. As it happens, it's very good. But that wasn't the point I was making.'

Then he permitted one corner of his mouth to pucker disparagingly. 'I don't intend remaking myself to suit you. What you see is what you get. If you want to scream, young lady, go ahead.'

Jane sighed, running her fingers through her thick, silky hair. 'I don't know what to make of you,' she said guardedly.

He narrowed his slaty eyes slightly. 'Don't you?'

'You're making me feel very uncomfortable.'

One dark brow flickered. 'Really?'

'Yes.'

She sighed, folding her hands tightly on the table. Any minute now he was going to start quizzing her about Garston's and she wasn't at all sure she would be able to handle it diplomatically. She decided to take the bull—tentatively—by the horns. 'Look...um...Guy, I don't understand what's going on. I don't understand why you've brought me out to lunch...perhaps if you could just get straight to the point we could save some of your precious time.' She tried to look severely at him, but was fairly sure that it wasn't working.

He certainly didn't look the least bit intimidated. One eyebrow curved sardonically. 'I'm paying court to you! I told you that.'

He'd said it again! She was sure her face must be blood-red, despite her colouring. And it wasn't even as if it were the truth...

'That's a very strange thing to say,' she muttered stiffly. 'People don't say things like that these days.'

'It's an explicit and accurate term. I like it.'

'Yes...but it isn't true.'

'Why shouldn't it be?'

'Because you're making no attempt to be nice to me for a start! If you really had asked me out because you...um...well, you know what I mean——'

'Because I fancy you?'

'Well, that isn't exactly the expression I would have chosen, but——'

'None the less, it, also, is explicit and accurate.'

'Yes, but... well, so is "finding someone attractive", for instance.'

Guy shrugged and pulled a face, the corners of his well-shaped mouth turning downwards. 'There are certain politicians I find attractive. I like their style. But I certainly don't fancy them. No, Jane Garston—saying that one finds someone attractive when, in truth, one fancies them, is no more than a euphemism. I'll stick with the vocabulary I choose, if you don't mind. That way there can be no mistakes.'

'Well, OK then. But it still doesn't alter the fact that you *don't* fancy me, because you're not... not...'

'Not smarming all over you? Good gracious, Jane, you do have a lot to learn about me! And before we go any further, let me assure you that I find you quite ravishing.'

Jane scowled and ran her tongue nervously over her lips. Ironically the compliment itself left her absolutely stone-cold. Because the trouble was, Jane *was* exceptionally beautiful. And, unfortunately, she had been told as much by so very many people over the years— probably by way of compensation for all the other things they declined to mention about her appearance—that the words had lost any power to move her. It was simply a fact, like her shoe-size.

'Don't you believe me?'

She nodded. 'I suppose so.'

'Why didn't you thank me for the compliment, then? You're so well-brought-up that I can hardly believe it was because you hadn't been taught that it was the correct way to respond.'

She sighed again. 'But I thought you liked straight talking?'

'I do,' he acknowledged with a flicker of his eyelids. 'So why don't you like to be told that you're beautiful?'

Jane hesitated. 'I don't mind being told that,' she admitted. 'It's the fatuous things that people follow on with I can't bear. *"So exotic"*,' she mimicked. '"Your complexion, my dear—pure *café au lait*"... Nobody's ever managed to tell me what the right response to comments like that should be. I mean how would they like it if I said, "commonplace" or "milky tea" about their faces?'

Guy smiled. 'You should try it and find out.'

Jane held back a laugh. 'It would be unkind,' she said honestly.

'Wouldn't they deserve it?'

'No. They're actually trying to be nice, after all. They're just...well...inept. Insensitive. That's all... It's my parents' set mostly...they're older and sort of stuffy. They just don't get it right.'

Guy didn't respond to that. He just leaned back in his chair and surveyed her very directly, making her feel more uncomfortable than ever.

'Can we change the subject?' she asked weakly.

'Be my guest.' His features were, as ever, composed, his eyes cool and appraising.

How did he manage to keep himself in check like that? Didn't he ever give anything away? She stared at him, transfixed, for a moment, and then struggled to gather her wits. Change the subject? Oh, yes. Of course. What he really wanted to talk about was the family firm, of course... Still, at least the ball was in her court. She could change it to something completely neutral. She took a deep breath and smiled. 'Do you live in the West Midlands?'

'No. I have several homes. Mostly I live in London when I'm in Britain.'

'Then you're just a visitor to the Black Country?'

'Not exactly...'

She'd ignore that one. He wanted her to ask what he was doing here, and that could only lead to one subject...

'You must take the opportunity to visit Stratford-upon-Avon, while you're in these parts. Oh, and Warwick and Dudley Castles and Coventry Cathedral...'

'Why? Except for Dudley, they're not particularly close.'

'Oh, they're not far. And they're all very impressive...'

'Are they, now...?'

'Yes.'

'Not exactly characteristic of the Black Country, though? It's the industrial landscape of the area which fascinates me...'

'Really?' she replied haughtily, feeling a little panicky as she sensed where the conversation was leading. 'I can't think why...anyway, Stratford and Warwick and so on... They're much older...more true to what the area was before...um...'

'Before the Industrial Revolution,' he completed for her. Then added ironically, 'Did you know that there's been coal-mining in these parts since the thirteenth century?'

'Oh...no...I hadn't realised that.' Then she found herself grinning impulsively. 'If that's true then Mum's family must have been even more stupid than we'd been giving them credit for. They used to be big landowners generations ago, you see. But in the last century they sold off land to the men who made a fortune from the iron and coal and clay and lime—and everything else that's in the ground here. We'd always figured that they must have been ignorant of its potential to have lost money here so spectacularly, at a time when everyone one else was busy making it. In the end they even sold the ancient family house, and had the one we live in built instead.' She laughed. 'That in itself shows an uncommon lack of judgement.'

'So you don't like your home?'

Jane sighed. That wasn't what she had meant. As it happened, she loved the old place—even if it was rather short on windows and dreadfully ugly. 'I didn't mean that,' she said bleakly. 'Honestly, I...um... It's just not a very beautiful house. That's all.'

'The one they sold was better, was it?'

'It's all a matter of taste,' she said uncomfortably, then, seeing another way to change the conversation, added, 'What would your dream house be like, Guy?'

He shrugged. 'I don't dream much these days. I have the money to turn dreams into decisions.'

'OK, but before...when you did dream...?'

Again he shrugged. 'Oh, I don't know. We're talking about a very long time ago...schoolboy stuff. Secret passages and big farmhouse kitchens with home-baked bread. That sort of thing.'

'Uh-huh...'

He was scrutinising her very keenly now. His inky eyes casting back and forth over her face.

There was a silence. Her stomach lurched a little. This was terrible. She really *must* change the subject again...

'London,' she said brightly. 'I love London.'

He shrugged. 'I don't spend much time there. I'm abroad quite a lot these days.'

'Oh...' She looked at him, puzzled. Right from the first moment she had noticed something indefinable about the way he spoke... Unusually, his voice betrayed nothing at all of his origins. Perhaps, she found herself speculating, he spoke English so perfectly because it wasn't his first language...? And his skin was quite olivey, even though his hair was no more than a very dark brown...? '*Are* you British?' she asked suspiciously.

He looked at her and then parted his lips in a very small smile. 'Indeed I am. As are you.'

Once again she felt as if his voice had flashed across the space between them to score her skin. 'That's not the assumption that most people make,' she replied archly.

He let his smile widen. 'Then you clearly mix with people who are not only inept and insensitive but ignorant, too. However obvious it may be that you have ancestral connections with some other part of the globe, you are now, and have been for most of your life I presume, the legal child of your parents. As both of them have long and prominent British pedigrees, then so do you.'

Jane couldn't help the quick rush of delight which greeted his remark. He had quite spontaneously said exactly what she had always felt. So many people assumed that because she looked so undeniably foreign that her personality, too, must bear traces of her origins. Yet she had only ever known one country—one family. She was her parents' child in every way that mattered. She gave a little sigh of relief, and relaxed a little. 'You don't have to keep your eyes *very* wide open to realise that I'm adopted,' she admitted ruefully.

'It is rather obvious,' he agreed, and this time his voice seemed reassuring and approving.

They seemed to have hit safe territory, at last. Suddenly he seemed so much more agreeable. Jane wrinkled her nose and laughed. 'Some people have very odd ideas about me,' she admitted confidingly. 'I once went to lunch with a family who served me rice and everyone else potatoes.'

Now it was his turn to laugh. It was the richest, deepest laugh she had ever heard, and, just as it had in the car, it filled her with an overwhelming sense of his humanity. All at once he seemed touchable, real, and yet still utterly unfathomable. The insight frightened her. She looked down at her hands.

'Which part of the globe do your original parents come from?' he asked bluntly.

Jane shook her head. 'I don't know for certain. Though I do know that I was born in Rio de Janeiro, so I think it's safe to presume they must be Brazilians. Though I've been told I don't look very Brazilian. I met an Argentinian once who said, ''Anywhere in the entire South American continent... but not Brazil!'' So I suppose you can take your pick.'

He leaned back in his chair and surveyed her. 'Have you never been back there to see for yourself?'

She shook her head.

He shrugged. 'I think I see what your friend was getting at. But Rio is about as cosmopolitan and diverse a city as one can imagine, and Brazil itself is a huge country, teeming with people from all over the place. You look like a bit of a mixture to me.'

'That's what she said,' agreed Jane.

'It makes sense,' he said speculatively. 'Those eyes of yours are almost entirely Inca—except perhaps that they're so large. But that oval face... the fine bone-structure...and your narrow nose...there could be Latin blood, too, perhaps? Certainly a combination of some sort—and there's undoubtedly plenty of mixed blood in Brazil. Your mouth is entirely Indian, though...'

Jane smiled very broadly, her full, tilted upper lip stretching wide to reveal her even white teeth. She was delighted by his directness. People pussy-footed around so much...it didn't take much to guess that she had been adopted from another country, but very few people had the nerve to enquire more deeply, which annoyed her because she was very proud of her unknown Brazilian ancestry. After all, if she hadn't been born in Rio at carnival time, just when the city was seething with tourists, she would never have ended up as Jane Garston, the beloved child of such wonderful parents. Just thinking about it made her eyes sting a little. She blinked furiously, annoyed with herself for being so hopelessly sentimental... 'I'm certainly very proud to be British now,' she said softly.

Guy nodded. 'How old were you when you became a Garston?'

'Ten months, officially, but really I was my parents' child from within an hour or so of my birth. They were in Rio for the carnival and they found me wrapped in rags, and abandoned on the steps of a small community of nuns who were often presented with unwanted children. Except that my parents didn't know that there was anything special about the doorstep where they found me. They thought it was just an ordinary house. They rang the doorbell, but of course, it being the middle of a religious festival, all the nuns were at Mass and no one answered.'

'So they just picked you up and took you home?'

'It wasn't quite that easy! First they took me back to their hotel-room and rang the police and summoned a doctor. But the police took ages coming, because of the carnival again, you see, and by the time they did arrive we'd had time to get to know each other and they'd fallen in love. It took ten months for the adoption to be arranged, but Mum stayed in Rio the whole time so that she could see me every day. I'd had to be placed in an orphanage in the circumstances, and it was quite a tricky matter getting the adoption arranged. But luckily it all came right in the end.'

'And you're an only child?'

'Yes. Mum and Dad had already applied to adopt in this country because they couldn't have children of their own. The trip to Rio was to be a sort of farewell to their childless life. When you think of all the millions of people in the city who could have found me, it was almost miraculous that it should have been them.'

Guy leaned back in his seat and surveyed her steadily. 'That's quite a history.'

Jane shrugged awkwardly. 'Yes,' she said in a small, brittle voice. In fact, she had an almost mystical belief in the rightness of what had happened. It was an impossible thing to explain to anyone except her parents, who shared her sense of wonder and awe. It certainly wasn't the sort of thing she could try to explain to a man like Guy. She looked flounderingly at him for a moment, wondering what to say next. Luckily the food arrived at that point and put paid to conversation for a while.

While Jane ate she tried her hardest to keep her eyes on the plate. But it wasn't easy. She found herself snatching quick glances at him all the time, and every time she did her stomach clenched and the food turned papery in her mouth. She found him unbelievably attractive—and not in the way she might find a politician attractive, either—if she ever managed to work up any interest in politics, that was... Put bluntly, she fancied him like mad. Jane began to feel distinctly annoyed with herself.

She felt even more annoyed with herself when Guy pushed his plate to one side and asked, 'Do you work for your father, Jane?'

Mug, she admonished inwardly. Talking about her origins had simply been a ploy to put her at her ease. 'No,' she said.

'Why not?'

'I don't want to.'

'So what do you do?'

'I do clerical work for a charity. When they need me, that is. It's a bit spasmodic.'

'Why don't you have a proper job?'

Jane winced. It would seem a bit sanctimonious to tell the truth—which was that she didn't need the money, and she felt she could do some good by being available to help out when the charity needed her. Especially as the charity concerned itself with finding homes for abandoned children. In a funny sort of way it helped her feel she was giving back some of her own incredible good luck. 'I'm not a career type,' she said brightly—which was, after all, also perfectly true.

'You've presumably had a good education, though?'

'Good enough,' she conceded cagily.

'But you didn't get the qualifications to work in your father's firm...' he said evenly.

'I could work there now if I wanted to. I've told you already—I work on and off for a charity. It's my own choice.'

'So what do you do with yourself the rest of the time?'

'I see friends. And I help my mother with the garden and the house, and with other charity work. She's always busy.'

'Is that all?'

'Look, Guy,' she muttered defensively. 'I'm only twenty-one. I haven't exactly had time yet to do millions of interesting and exciting things with my life.'

'So what *are* all these interesting and exciting things you have planned?'

Jane sighed. In all honesty, she didn't know. She had always been too contented with life just as it was to hanker after more. She had certainly never been possessed by any raging ambitions—a fact which occasioned her the odd pang of guilt. So many young women these days seemed to be single-minded go-getters. She couldn't help feeling a bit inadequate now and then. But really, no matter how much soul-searching she did, she couldn't find a shred of that hunger in herself. She wanted, really...oh, she just wanted to be like her mother—kind and thoughtful, doing what little good it came her way to do, hurting no one and always finding something to amuse her within the narrow parameters of her life. 'I don't know,' she said helplessly. 'I just want to enjoy life to the full. That's all.'

'So you're not planning to take over Garston's when your father retires?'

Jane shook her head angrily. It was so obvious where all these innocent lines of questioning were leading. Why was she bothering to answer him at all? 'No,' she snapped decisively. 'I don't know anything about engineering—or business come to that.'

'You could learn.'

'Oh, no, I couldn't!' she exclaimed, horrified. She had often been taken to the works as a child, but the place had appalled her. The big lathes and milling machines had petrified her for a start. She had hated it. Perhaps it also had something to do with the fact that her father had always made her wear goggles? They had smelt of rubber and sat heavily on the small bones of her face, making her feel as if she would suffocate. 'We don't want you to risk getting a bit of swarf in your eyes,' he used to say kindly, indicating the curling shreds of metal which flew from the huge machines. She used to have nightmares about swarf... Something about a monster with curly metal hair wearing goggles... She shuddered at the recollection even now, and felt her face tugging into a small grimace. 'Horrible place,' she muttered under her breath. Her father used to have to carry her, pale and trembling, back to the car, teasing her gently and promising ice-creams.

Guy's eyes seemed to be watching her with a peculiar detachment. No doubt he thought he could glean something of her father's long-term plans for the business by enquiring into Jane's involvement.

'I shan't be taking over the running of the family firm...' she said decisively. 'It's utterly pointless talking to me about it. I know nothing about it and I don't want to know. I don't even own a single share in it. And I have no desire to talk about engineering in any way, shape or form. So that's that. We can talk about something else starting right now or you can take me home.' She folded her arms and forced herself to meet his eye.

Damn him. For once his features had allowed themselves to betray his thoughts. Annoyance bit at the corners of his mouth, and his eyes were as hard as steel. He glanced pointedly at his watch. 'We'll do without coffee,' he said coolly. 'I don't want to be late.'

Well, there was no fooling herself about what that meant. No information on the firm meant no more of his precious time being wasted. Jane swallowed hard, and collected her anorak which had been draped over the back of her chair. She stood up, drawing herself up to her full five feet six, and holding her chin high. 'Please don't let *me* detain you,' she said tightly.

Guy tilted his chair back and folded his arms, watching her as she slipped her arms into the sleeves, moving away from him to one side of the table. He let a small, cynical smile play around his mouth. Otherwise he didn't move a muscle.

Her stomach was still knotty, and her consciousness of him as a man—a very attractive man—was still in full flood. Ugh. Chemistry. Like courtship, it was an old-fashioned word—but no less explicit and accurate for all that. Determined not to betray her own inner sense of humiliation, she dropped her head to fumble with the zip of her anorak. When she had zipped it right up to the neck she found he was still watching her in that disdainful way. She stuck her hands in her pockets and tossed her head.

'Come on,' she said. 'I thought you were in a hurry?'

His smile widened slightly. Then he glanced at his watch again. 'I can spare a further two minutes,' he said. 'I shall use them up looking at you.'

Jane felt the warmth of embarrassment creep up her neck as she stood staunchly, waiting.

At last he unfolded his lean frame, dropped a banknote on to the table and got to his feet. He put one hand casually on her shoulder and began to move towards the door.

'Get your hands off me,' she hissed.

He let his hand drop. 'Fair enough,' he commented drily. 'I take it I'm to be made to wait a little longer for my invitation? No sweat. I can wait.'

There was no way she was going to reply to that one! Jane shook her hair back from her face and walked briskly to the door. She kept her arms folded and said nothing during the short drive back. When he dropped her off outside her front door she got out of the car as fast as she could.

'Thank you for lunch,' she muttered as politely as she could manage. 'I enjoyed it.'

Guy was leaning across the passenger seat to pull her door closed. He tilted his head wryly. That mole—neither large nor small, darkish brown, set just below the proud angle of his cheekbone—caught her eye once more. Again he looked quite beautiful. Again her stomach clenched in recognition of the effect the image had on her senses.

'Good,' he said automatically. His eyes met hers then looked away. 'I'll be in touch,' he added coldly.

CHAPTER THREE

HE WOULDN'T. She knew that beyond a shadow of doubt. He didn't like her, and she knew nothing that would be of use to him, so he would not, under any circumstances, get in touch with her.

Ironically, this knowledge did not stop Jane from jumping out of her skin every time the phone rang. Nor did it stop her from re-running their conversations in her head, nor from thinking that she could see a black Lotus disappearing around every bend when she was out of doors. She felt sick with herself. And, of course, he didn't get in touch.

Matters weren't helped when her father, made nervous by a a call from a distant cousin revealing that somebody was showing an interest in her few shares, decided to invite Guy to their home for a meal.

'You're crazy, Dad,' she accused.

Her father smiled benignly. 'I'm not. If he's going to gobble me up, the sooner he gets a taste for me the better. Anyway, I admire what I've seen of the man. If he does buy Garston's I'd like to think I could get on well with him.'

'You're a saint,' she sighed.

'A pragmatist,' he returned firmly, then added kindly, 'Why worry about it, Janey? Just be happy, huh? That's all your mother and I have ever wanted for you.'

Jane hadn't said much to her parents about her encounters with Guy. She thought it might muddy the waters if they felt they had to be loyal to her feelings in the middle of all this. So she prayed that he wouldn't

39

accept the invitation. When he did accept, the first thing she found herself doing was searching through her wardrobe for the right thing to wear. Disgusted beyond belief she almost cheered with relief when her friend Charlotte rang and offered an alternative itinerary for the evening.

'We'll have to drive within fifteen miles of your place, so it will be no trouble to stop by and pick you up,' she said. 'I'll tell Rory you're coming, so you needn't feel like a gatecrasher. And anyway, Benedicta and Rupert want you to come, so you must.'

'OK. OK. I'll come . . . I only mentioned the dinner because . . . well, never mind. This party of Rory's sounds brilliant. I'll see you about eightish tomorrow.'

She knew her parents were hurt that she wasn't going to be there, but honestly, the way things were she'd do more harm than good by remaining. She was doing them a favour by going out. She defied Guy to dislike her parents if he was left on his own with them.

That was what she kept telling herself as she dressed in a drapey black dress with shoe-string straps and waited in the gloomy hall for the twins—Charlotte and Benedicta—and their brother Rupert to show up.

Naturally they were late. Guy hadn't arrived by the time the red Range Rover pulled up and her friends spilled out, but it was going to be a close-run thing. Jane was feeling decidedly jumpy.

'Jane, you look gorgeous!' exclaimed Benedicta. 'I wish we hadn't suggested you come now. Charlie and I will look like a pair of old frumps beside you,'

Benedicta could only afford to say this because it was manifestly untrue. Even had the twins not been so pretty, the amount of flesh they were exposing would ensure that however they were classified, it would not be as frumps.

Jane grabbed her coat and bag and headed straight for the car. 'Come on,' she muttered. 'Let's not hang around.'

Charlie yawned. 'There's no rush. I'm stiff after driving up from Sussex. Let's go in and say hello to your mother.'

'Let's not,' said Jane briskly. 'She's entertaining to-night. She's busy. Some other time, huh?'

'Oh, yes. You mentioned it on the phone. Some associate of your father's you said . . . Who is he? Anyone we know?'

At which point, to Jane's horror, the black Lotus swerved in through the gates and began swooping up the driveway towards them like a hungry locust.

'Guy Rexford,' admitted Jane, clambering swiftly into the back and praying the others would follow.

The Lotus swung past them to the parking bay behind the hedge. The others did not follow her into the Range Rover. They stood languidly on the driveway, looking young and beautiful and enjoying the spring evening— and making very sure they got a good look at whoever was driving that expensive black car.

Rupert stuck his head through the door and grinned at her. 'Blimey, Jane! You mean you're passing up an evening with Mr Wonderful to come out with *us*? Hey, girls, did you hear that?'

The twins had. They too stuck their heads round the door. 'He's the one who's made all that money, isn't he?' they said, peering accusingly at Jane. 'We know all about him.'

The crunch of feet on gravel had the twins exchanging meaningful glances. Then Benedicta clambered in beside Jane and slammed the door shut, while Charlotte took a few steps towards Guy, who was even now appearing around the hedge. What were those two up to? And, oh, lord, why did he have to look so stunningly *mature*?

One of the problems with being twenty-one was that one had twenty-one-year-old friends. Friends who, Jane knew from experience, could behave as if they were half that age at times. She wondered, not for the first time, why the Berrington girls had befriended her so eagerly. She wasn't a bit like them, really.

'I'd better get out and say hello,' said Jane uncomfortably, her voice low.

But Benedicta shook her head. 'Why bother?' she said scornfully. 'After all, it's not as if you know him, is it?'

'I do, actually,' Jane admitted, watching Charlotte tilt her chin and smile coyly, and say something to Guy with a giggle. His features, of course, were unreadable as he replied, but she could guess that he wasn't impressed.

'He took me out to lunch last week, in fact,' Jane whispered, anxious to distract herself from the excruciating little spectacle taking place beyond the windscreen. 'Not that I'm seeing him again. I don't really like him.'

Benedicta pulled a face. 'I don't blame you. Yuk. Guy Rexford. Jumped-up so-and-so. I mean who is he? Who are his people?'

Jane was shocked. 'Joking aside, Benny, I didn't exactly see eye to eye with him,' she said courteously, giving the other girl a chance to retract.

But Benedicta merely shrugged. 'Of course not. How could you? You're worlds apart. He comes from some dump up north, for a start. It would be impossible to see eye to eye with someone like him. What Daddy can't understand is, who lent him the money to get *started*? None of Daddy's friends in the big merchant banks did, that's for sure. He says he must have got it by gambling, because he started out without a penny——'

'Benedicta, are you serious?' interrupted Jane abruptly, finding a rare, white anger beginning to boil inside her. At the same time she felt cold with shock that someone she had thought she knew could be saying things like this. About *anyone*. Not just Guy... though the fact that she was daring to say it when the man in question—a man so obviously capable of doing whatever he wanted in life without the patronage of Benedicta's father's friends—was standing just yards away, was particularly offensive. How *dared* she say such things? How dared she?

'Why shouldn't I be serious?' queried Benedicta. 'The man has no background whatsoever. I mean, anybody can make money these days, but the thing is——'

'Shut up,' hissed Jane under her breath. Luckily, Guy had turned on his heel and was mounting the steps to the house. The moment he had gone in she would jump out of this car and clear off in her own. Anything to get away from people who held views like that! Thankfully, the front door opened and he stepped inside.

Jane jumped out of the car. She turned a sickened expression on Benedicta. 'Do apologise to Rory for me,' she said in a choked voice, 'but I shan't be coming to the party after all.'

'Jane!' protested Benedicta indignantly.

Charlotte ran over and blocked Jane's path. 'Come on,' she said stiffly. 'Get back in. We're a bit late. If you've forgotten something I can always lend it to you.'

'I'm not coming,' said Jane, her voice shaking with fury. 'Your sister has just been telling me what she thinks of my parents' guest——'

'Oh, Rexford?' interrupted Charlotte casually. 'He's an oik, isn't he?'

'That's pretty much what Benedicta said,' returned Jane disgustedly, her dark eyes blazing. 'Now if you'll kindly get out of my way, Charlotte——'

The girl shrugged. 'But why should you care——?'

'I care not to be seen in the company of people like you. That's all you need to know,' returned Jane angrily.

Rupert grabbed her arm as she strode away. 'Jane. Please... I'm sure they didn't mean anything...' he insisted.

Jane looked into his anxious eyes. 'Sorry, Rupert, but if they didn't mean it, then they shouldn't have said it.' And she struggled to drag her arm free, but he wouldn't let go.

Under other circumstances she would have kept her cool and demanded that he let go of her arm in a civilised manner. But the sense of being trapped tipped her over some inner precipice and her temper fled.

'Let go!' she yelled, shaking her arm and throwing him off. 'I don't know what your thoughts on the matter are, Rupert, but if you don't let me go this instant I shall be forced to assume that *you* think that someone's breeding is all that counts, as well. Good grief! I'm astonished that you've consented to be seen in my company at all. After all, who are *my* people? What is *my* background? If that's the way you think, what the hell are you doing going to parties with someone like me?'

And then, to her horror, another hand came to rest on her beleaguered arm and a crisp, cold voice said, 'Jane Garston... fighting in the streets? Whatever next?'

Jane was shaking now. Her mind was blurred with rage. She flapped Guy's arm away, enraged even further by the powerful effect of his touch on her chemically activated senses.

'Leave me alone!' she bit out.

He crooked one eyebrow drily. 'I've just come out to fetch a journal from the car,' he said evenly. 'I'd promised to show it to your father, and I forgot to take it in with me. Now, why don't you come with me and sit in my car until you've calmed down? You can tell me what it's all about if it would make you feel better.'

Jane struggled to regain control of her breathing. She couldn't go into the house like this. And she was damned if she'd go anywhere with those wretched Berringtons. But if she tried to march off, one or other of them would try to stop her and she'd end up losing her cool again, and goodness only knew what might be said then. She couldn't bear the idea of Guy discovering what those awful, stuck-up Berringtons thought of him. It was too insulting to be borne.

'I . . .' She glanced at Rupert and the twins, who had backed away and were looking gratifyingly sheepish. 'My friends are just going,' she said stiffly. Then she turned back to Guy and said, 'Thank you,' in a small, tight voice, before walking, straight-backed, to his car.

He bleeped the car lock with his remote control so that she could get in, while he stood, arms folded, watching the Berringtons get into the Range Rover and drive off.

The moment she was in Guy's car her chin began to crumple. She bit hard on her lip. By the time Guy had got in beside her, she was fighting the desire to howl like a baby.

He sat in silence for a few minutes while she sniffed and blinked resolutely. She was damned if she'd break down in front of him. It might have been different if he'd liked her, but as things were she wouldn't give him the satisfaction.

'Do you want to let it out?' he said softly at last.

She tried to smile, but her mouth went all over the place, so she just shook her head.

He took a neatly ironed white handkerchief out of one pocket and offered it to her. 'You could try,' he said gently.

Again she shook her head, sniffing and swallowing at the same time, and nudging away a couple of renegade tears with one finger.

'You've been very badly hurt,' he said levelly at last. 'Haven't you?'

Jane gave an awkward little shrug. Then she blinked hard and managed a muffled, 'No.'

'Disappointed, then?'

She shook her head again. This was dreadful. She could hardly tell him that she'd been defending him . . . 'It was nothing,' she said stoically. 'I'm just over-reacting.'

'I heard a little of what was said,' he replied. 'I don't think you were over-reacting at all.'

Jane raised one hand to her ear and began rotating the gold ring. 'Well, *I* think I was,' she muttered defensively. 'I didn't like what they said, but I shouldn't have allowed myself to get so upset by it. I'm being stupid.'

There was a pause. Then Guy said in a steady, unemotional voice, 'I remember one Christmas when I was just a lad . . . I didn't have the usual sort of family Christmases, you see . . . But this one year—well, I woke up and there was no stocking for me. And I knew it was stupid to mind because I already knew there wasn't a Santa Claus, but I felt as though I was the only person in the whole world who hadn't been invited to some big party. It was as if everyone else had been allowed to join in, except me. I think that was the bleakest moment of my life. But I was determined not to let anyone else know how I felt, and so I kept up a brave face. Now, when I look back on that day I see it not as something bad, but as a source of strength. That was the day I learned to rely on myself.'

Jane turned a startled gaze on him. 'I . . . um . . .' She faltered, not knowing what to say. He was telling her that he could take people like the Berringtons in his stride . . . that he didn't need her to defend him. She admired him for putting it so tactfully. 'I see . . .' she said weakly.

He smiled a detached smile. 'Now come on in. I'm
sure your mother will be able to make the meal stretch
to four. You can tell them that you didn't like the sound
of this party and that you wisely decided not to go.
They'll be delighted.'

Of course they were. And of course the meal stretched
to four. And of course Guy was utterly charming and
even managed to disengage himself from a lively dis-
cussion on modern micrometers to ask her mother about
the garden. Jane sat quietly, feeling as if she were the
only person in the whole world who'd not been invited
to join in. You'd never have guessed it, though. She
smiled brightly and relied on herself.

When he left he put his hand lightly on her elbow and
said, 'I'll be in touch.'

The phone rang seven times the next day. None of the
calls was for her.

When a fortnight had gone by she decided she had
forgotten him almost completely, and was so eager to
get away from the wretched phone that she was actually
pleased when her poor mother bruised her toes with a
spade and she had to accompany her father to some
manufacturing industry function in Birmingham. But
when she spotted Guy standing in a corner, talking intently to a bald man with side-whiskers, and looking
taller and bigger than anybody else there, she
remembered that she hadn't forgotten him at all. His
left side was on view. The side with the mole. And he
was laughing now, that rich, melodic laugh which she
couldn't possibly be hearing across all the babble of
voices. And yet she was sure she was.

She ignored him completely. Luckily her father's
golfing pal, William Gresham—big in plastics, as he liked
reminding people—was standing near by and was only
too delighted to have a young beauty in a flame-coloured
dress start chattering animatedly to him. Jane knew him

well enough to know that golf and plastics would keep
him engaged in conversation for ages and ages. She had
underestimated it. By the time he had finished describing
his new flexible polymer, Jane was wishing she hadn't
accepted the third spritzer—and Guy Rexford was nowhere to be seen.

Good. She managed to excuse herself politely and
bolted off in search of the ladies'. She was almost there
when he reappeared.

'Jane Garston...' he said slowly. 'Well, well...'

She turned her large, almost black eyes directly on
his. Her heart was pounding with...with chemistry and
all her brain cells seemed to have coalesced into a heavy
lump. Only her bladder still seemed to be working
properly. 'Hello,' she said coolly, letting her eyebrows
lift with what she hoped was suitable disdain and crossing
her legs.

He ran the tip of his tongue across his lips. His eyes
were navy blue in the subdued lighting, his lashes short
and black and dense. 'I've been in Kuala Lumpur,' he
said briefly. 'I flew back in this morning.'

'Really?' Actually, he *was* incredibly tanned. Much
browner than he had been two weeks earlier. Her bladder
practically fizzed at the sight. She pressed her knees
together. 'I can't imagine what that's got to do with me.'

'Can't you? Then you haven't been wondering whether
I'd call you and ask you out again? You don't see it as
some kind of explanation?'

'No. Not at all.'

He looked down on her and his eyes seemed to be
laughing, even though his mouth was enigmatically
straight. 'Is that so? Now run along, Jane Garston...
quickly... Don't let me keep you waiting...' he said wryly,
lifting one eyebrow, and then adding, 'I'll be in touch.'

Either his patent amusement or his final comment—
she couldn't be sure which—gave her such a jolt that
she hardly dared uncross her legs. Certainly there was
no question of her airily dismissing him and swanning
off across the huge room, which was exactly what she
wanted to do. Instead, she hurriedly took the few ig-
nominious steps which separated her from the door to
the powder room, her skin burning and tears of mortification stinging her eyes. Of course, as soon as the
door closed behind her all the urgency disappeared, and
she was left facing her own dismal reflection in the large
mirror, and the discovery that this time, at least, her
blush was very visible indeed despite the golden hue of
her skin. She started to splash cold water on her face to
make it subside, but the sound of running water proved
too much for her automatic nervous system. She had to
rush for the cubicle, still red in the face and still blinking
away tears of mortification . . .

Back in front of the mirror she forced herself to face
the fact that whether she liked it or not she was absolutely obsessed with the man. He'd promised to get in
touch and he hadn't, and it was no good him making
excuses about being in Kuala Lumpur because they had
telephones in Kuala Lumpur, didn't they? He'd tried to
use her. He was planning to take over Garston's, and he
was making a worried man of her darling father, and
now he'd gone and said he'd get in touch again, and of
course he *wouldn't* and she'd waste another fortnight of
her life jumping out of her skin every time the phone
rang. Her blushes subsided to the point where she looked
positively pale.

She clenched her fists. She had to do something. She
had to do something which would ensure that she didn't
waste another hour of her life *fancying* him and
fantasising about him, and which might also get him off
her father's back—if he had a shred of common decency

in him, that was—which he didn't, because no man who would let his eyes tell you that he knew you were bursting to go to the loo could be counted as the least bit *decent*. None the less she could try.

She walked out of the powder room in exactly the manner she wished she'd walked into it. Chin high, eyes flashing, she set off to find him and give him a piece of her mind.

CHAPTER FOUR

AT LAST she caught a glimpse of the back of his head. He was disappearing out of the hotel reception area and through the main door. Swept along by anger, she broke into a run, pushing her way through the sedate groups of people in her path. When she caught up with him he was striding across the car park towards the low, dark shape of his car.

'Guy!' she shouted, her voice sounding shrill and thin in the night air.

He stopped and turned to look at her. Then he stood still, and waited for her to approach. 'I want a word with you,' she continued breathlessly, anxious that he shouldn't be the one to start talking and throw her off her stride.

'Yes?' His arms folded themselves slowly across the powerful expanse of his chest.

She gave a sudden shiver as she drew nearer. It was chilly out, and the short puff sleeves of her taffeta dress had brought goosebumps up on her arms. She crossed her own arms and hugged herself. 'It's about our firm,' she said emphatically, fearful that if she didn't spill the words out quickly her nerve would fail her. 'I've come to tell you to leave it alone.'

'Garston's?'

'The very one,' she bit out sarcastically. 'Look, it's *ours*. Can you understand that? My grandfather's grandfather or my father's great-great-grandfather or...or someone like that founded it, and it's gone from father to son ever since. I *know* that there are shares all over the place and there shouldn't be. But that's only because of Aunt Florrie and the cats' home.'

'What the hell are you talking about?'

Her anger flared anew. 'Oh, don't pretend to be so innocent! We know perfectly well that you're planning to take it over.'

'Am I?'

'Of course you are. Do you think we're stupid? We know someone's trying to buy shares.'

'That doesn't mean that the firm's about to be taken over. Simply that someone's taking an interest.'

'That someone being you.'

He didn't respond directly. He simply said. 'Garston's are almost ready to market their new gearing system. Any one of a number of people could be very interested in having a stake in that.'

Jane looked at him blankly for a moment and then said in a low, fierce voice, 'No. If that was what was going on, Dad would know. He knows everything about Garston's. He loves that place, you know? He lives and breathes it. He's devoted his life to it, and he's always been contented and happy and now he's worried to death and it's all your fault. Why can't you just leave the place alone? It's profitable. Dad obviously manages it well. And before you say anything else, I know he should have bought Aunt Florrie's shares himself but he's always too busy reinvesting to spare money for himself...Mum even makes her own curtains.' She took a deep gulp of the raw evening air. 'It's not fair,' she finished, her voice cracking a little with emotion. 'You've got *everything*. Why do you have to come along and take away everything we have, too?'

The car park was floodlit. Guy's shirt-front looked very white as he unfolded his arms and took a few steps towards her. His eyes glittered and looked densely black and dangerous as he moved closer to her. Oh, lord—

she'd really gone and torn it now. A man like him
wouldn't like being told what he could and couldn't do
with his business empire by a young woman like her.
Wouldn't like it one bit. Her eyes filled with tears of
frustration.

And then, to her astonishment, his hands came out
and bit into her shoulders, his head dropped swiftly
towards hers and he began to kiss her. He kissed her
with a ferocity which took her breath away. His mouth
opened over hers determinedly, his tongue strong against
her lips. He tasted salty and male. Shock-waves rocked
her, but she didn't pull away from him. She had watched
his mouth, transfixed, when he had spoken to her, and
somewhere—way beneath the lapping and splashing of
her conscious mind—a dark curiosity had ducked and
dived. She had wanted to know how it would be to be
kissed by that mouth. Now she was finding out.

And the answer to her question was heady stuff indeed.
It was like nothing else she had ever known. His mouth
felt right against hers. It felt as if it belonged there, and
had always done so and could never belong anywhere
else. Slowly, fluttering a little, her eyes closed and she
found herself sinking into the world of that kiss. And
it wasn't just her mouth that slipped so eagerly into this
heaven, either; all her senses followed with alarming
rapidity. Within short minutes she was kissing him back
with a frantic urgency, crushing the taffeta of her bodice
as she clung to him, moving and arching so that her
breasts thrust against his crisp shirt-front, thrilling to
the power of the lean male flesh beyond.

Arousal flamed inside her, scorching her nerve-
endings, forcing her even closer against him. Then Guy's
hand came down to find a breast, making her breath
catch roughly in her throat. His fingers cupped the mass
while his thumb tracked back and forth along the edge
of her bodice, dusting the silken swell of her skin with

prickling sensation. Unconsciously, she let out her breath
so that her body hollowed a little, freeing fabric from
flesh by a fraction, and seeming to beg his thumb to
intrude between silk and skin and find the hot nub of
her breast for itself. And eagerly his thumb took up the
invitation. It travelled decisively inside her dress and
burrowed beneath the lace of her bra, clambering
tantalisingly over and around her hard, excited nipple.

Their mouths tore apart as Jane gasped aloud her astonished pleasure. Her eyes flew wide with delight as she
greeted the needle-sharp darts of desire which assailed
her. She could see nothing for a moment, and then her
vision cleared and she saw, blurred and shadowy in the
darkness, his white collar, the hard angular shape of his
jaw, and above—darker and even more shadowy—the
hollows of his eyes. Eyes which, although she couldn't
see them now, seemed eternally to be masking their disapproval of her. Eyes set in a face which had schooled
itself to give nothing away. Suddenly Jane was frightened
of this man. How on earth had he induced her to behave
so shamelessly? What was it about him?

With a burst of panicky resolution Jane fought free
of his arms. 'What did you have to go and do that for?'
she muttered querulously. 'I told you not to touch me.
I thought you said you'd wait to be invited?'

He smiled, his teeth flashing white in the cold, blue
light. 'I figured you weren't very likely to issue that invitation in the circumstances. So I decided to gatecrash.'

Jane had never felt so confused or humiliated in all
her life. Her mouth still felt bruised and swollen from
his embrace. She had given herself to it so wantonly,
even though it had been no more than a display of raw,
male power on his part. He had simply wanted to put
her in her place—and what better way to emphasise the
fact that he despised her than by kissing her? And she,
fool that she was, had lapped it up. She rubbed her

mouth with the back of her hand. 'I don't know how you dared...' she muttered.

'It was easy, Jane. And anyway, you loved it. Where's the problem?'

'The problem is that I didn't want you to. I told you not to touch me once before, and I thought you might respect that. But you're not the type of man who bothers with little things like respect, are you? You've no respect for my father's life—and even less for me. I'm just a woman. A young woman. I don't count, do I?'

'Jane, was that the first time you'd been kissed?'

She eyed him suspiciously, looking up through the dark shadow of her fringe, with eyes, which if she only knew it, were huge and lambent. 'No. Of course not. But I'm not the sort of girl you seem to think I am.' Her eyes took on a new defiance. 'I'm a virgin, as it happens,' she added grittily.

Still his features registered nothing. 'Jane, I kissed you, that's all. You liked it. I didn't violate you. I did it on impulse—which was how I'd always assumed such things were meant to be done. I wasn't even aware that it was possible to book kisses in advance—or were all your other kisses undertaken by appointment only?'

An image of the eager faces of Jane's former boyfriends swam in front of her eyes. 'The other men who kissed me weren't like you,' she complained. 'They were a different type of man. It was... different.'

'But not better,' he said confidently, and suddenly his face broke into one of its unexpectedly broad smiles. With a flash of panic she realised that he was about to laugh.

She couldn't bear to hear him laugh. His laughter made him whole. It made him real, and yet at the same time utterly alien. His eyes narrowed and sparkled. He *was* going to laugh...

She laid the palms of her hands against his broad chest and pushed hard. He didn't budge, but he did start to laugh. Furious, charged with a mixture of desire and despair, she pushed harder, so that her arms straightened and her features crumpled with the effort. Apart from the rhythmic quaking of his chest he still didn't move. Wild now with the power of her need, she dropped her head and pushed using every ounce of her strength. He remained as solid as a rock. Then all of a sudden he stopped laughing and caught hold of her around the waist and swung her up in the air, setting her down again, closer to him.

'Why did you do that?' she complained desperately.

His shoulders lifted slightly. 'If I'd moved away you would have fallen flat on your face. It seemed the kinder option.'

She tugged away from him and took a few steps backwards. 'Go away,' she muttered shakily. 'Just go away.'

His eyes shone. 'Very well,' he growled slowly. 'But I'll be in touch, Jane Garston. You can be sure of that.'

She stared at him in shock for a moment. She'd come out here to try to anger him. To irritate and annoy him. So that he'd never make any more of his empty promises to be in touch. So that she could kill her own obsession with him stone-dead. And yet she had achieved the complete opposite. He was still promising to be in touch, only now her body was craving his touch so powerfully that when the promise was broken, as it surely would be, it would be quite impossible for her to put him out of her mind. And no doubt he was more determined than ever to go ahead with the take-over.

He would do exactly as he pleased. That was the message the kiss had been intended to deliver. She turned on her heel and ran back to the golden rectangle of light beneath the striped awning. She ran up the steps and through the plate glass door and back into the hotel.

In the car on the way back she asked, 'Why was Bill Gresham surprised to see Guy Rexford there, Dad?'

Her father shrugged his shoulders. 'He doesn't socialise much. In fact, everyone was speculating as to which firm in this area he was planning to buy. I didn't confess that it was mine.'

'Is he so predictable?'

'Business-wise, yes. He bought up his first company when he was very young—twenty or so. And he's just kept going ever since—always engineering firms—and always good ones. He certainly knew what he was up to from the start—and yet no one knows where he got his capital or his expertise. It's rumoured that he came from a very modest background. Anyway, he's made an international name for himself now. Whatever his background might once have been, he left it behind a long time ago. It certainly hasn't done him any harm.'

Nothing, she thought, could harm him. He *had* violated her, no matter that he had only kissed her. And yet he himself was inviolable.

This time the fortnight seemed far longer. And this time Jane couldn't fool herself that she didn't care. The kiss would not let itself be forgotten. It drowned her dreams. It nudged at the edges of her mind all day long, no matter how busy she tried to keep herself. It swamped her as she sat in front of the television, watching actors and actresses pretend to kiss, and wondering how they could bear to tolerate the pretence when the reality could be so special.

Her father's face was also a constant reminder of the power of Guy Rexford to disturb. Someone had bought the cats' home shares. And a second cousin had sold out too—and why should he not have been tempted at prices like that? There was no pretending now that it might never happen. It was going to happen. The only question was when.

At six o'clock on a Thursday evening the telephone
rang.

'Jane?'

Her heart leapt. 'Who is that speaking?'

'Don't pretend you don't know. I'll pick you up at
seven-thirty.'

'No.'

'Dress up. I'll take you somewhere nice for a meal.'
And with that the phone went dead.

Jane dressed up. Her fingers shook as she applied her
frugal dusting of make-up. Her stomach churned and
knotted and her mouth was so dry she couldn't swallow.
She was going. She was going because . . . because she
might be able, even now at the eleventh hour, to persuade him not to continue with his take-over.

She tapped herself angrily on the forehead. Fat chance!
Who was she kidding? She had played all her cards as
far as Garston's was concerned. She had no business
knowledge with which to call his bluff. So *why* was she
going? She knew nothing at all about him, except that
he was ruthless and he fancied her, and yet here she was,
bathing in scented water and blow-drying her hair to an
elegant, glossy finish, dabbing perfume on her pulse-
points and stepping into the most subtle of all the dresses
in her wardrobe, and her hands were trembling and she
was even now pouring herself a small sherry to steady
her nerves. She couldn't for the life of her understand
why she was doing all these things.

Of course, when he arrived, looking devastating in a
charcoal suit and a broad-striped lilac and white silk
shirt, she knew exactly why. To her dismay he sought
out her parents before they left.

'Sidney . . . Wendy . . . good to see you again.' And he
offered his strong, brown hand to be shaken with
an air of such good-humoured frankness that Jane
wanted to scream.

She had deliberately not told her parents who her escort was to be—hoping to slip out unnoticed while they watched television. Now her blood curdled with shame as she watched her parents, stiff smiles in place, having to take the proffered hand. Her parents were far too nice and polite to upset the apple cart, but she was sure that it must be agony for them.

'I'm taking Jane out to dinner. I'm afraid I gave her very little notice. I hope it hasn't upset your plans for eating this evening?'

'Not at all...not at all...' muttered her father generously.

Jane swallowed. 'We'd better get going,' she said a little too loudly. Then, 'Don't wait up for me...' And with that she pointedly made her way out into the hall. She heard Guy's voice murmur a parting remark but didn't pause to catch what he was saying. Instead she walked briskly to the front door, her heels clacking on the stone floor. He caught up with her at the door, reaching across her to open it, and taking her arm as he led her outside and handed her into the car.

'What shall we talk about?' he asked with that rough-edged directness which so discomfited her.

'Why should I care? You can choose the subject,' she replied defensively.

He sighed. It was the first time she had heard him sigh, and it wasn't a pleasant experience. She felt insulted by it.

He said nothing more throughout the long drive. Jane turned her head time and again to glance at him. His eyes remained resolutely fixed on the road ahead. To her dismay she discovered she was more excited by his presence than she would have thought possible. Absence had not neutralised the chemicals. Far from it. His physical proximity proved the ultimate catalyst. She wanted to cry.

He took her to a very exclusive restaurant overlooking the Avon at Warwick. She shivered as he took her coat from her and flesh brushed tantalisingly against flesh.

When he admired her green halter-neck dress, claiming that it showed her shoulders and back to perfection, she was tremblingly relieved that she had worn something with a high neck.

'The dress must have been designed for you,' he said.

'You couldn't be more wrong,' she snapped back, frightened by the animal pleasure his approval was generating in her. 'It's pure serendipity. The dress came from a chain store.'

The waiter arrived with heavy, leather-bound menus. Jane hid behind hers.

'What will you have?' Guy asked eventually.

'Um ... I haven't decided.'

'Jane, you've been looking at that menu for ages. What's the matter?'

She laid the menu down on the table in front of her. 'I wish I hadn't come,' she said, her miserable face betraying her confusion. 'I can't concentrate on the menu. I just keep thinking that I wish I hadn't come.'

'Shall I order for you?' he asked.

She shook her head. 'I think you'd better take me home. You didn't give me much option about coming— and anyway, I seem to do what you tell me, whether I like it or not. Though I suppose I could just have refused to open the door. But I wouldn't have wanted to cause a scene and attract my parents' attention. Look, I ... I didn't want them to know I'd had anything to do with you since you came to dinner. It was a month ago, after all.'

She stopped for a moment, looking down at the white damask cloth and the heavy silverware in front of her. When she looked up Guy was watching her attentively.

'I don't know how you could have done it,' she burst out wretchedly. 'I don't know how you could have marched into their sitting-room and made them shake hands with you and be polite to you, when all along you were wheeling and dealing behind their backs and planning to ruin their lives.'

Guy looked at her very steadily. 'I had a very good reason for introducing myself to your parents tonight,' he said evenly.

'Yes. So that you could size up my father and see whether he'll be worth keeping on—or whether you'll need to force him out.'

Guy shook his head. 'I'm not going to take over Garston's.'

'I don't believe you. Why should I?'

'Because I say so.'

'Huh! You said you wouldn't touch me without my say-so—and yet you did.'

'Ah, that was different. I couldn't resist you, Jane. I was overwhelmed by your attractions.'

'Rot. Anyway, I thought "attraction" wasn't a sufficiently explicit and accurate word for you?'

He laughed. 'Well, OK. But usually I'm a man of my word. As long as the temptations aren't too great.'

'Oh, Guy, you must think I'm an infant! You're a sharp businessman. I may not be very experienced but I do know that you don't get to be as successful as *you* are without treading on a few toes.'

Guy shrugged. 'You know nothing about me, Jane.'

'You've never told me anything about yourself.'

'You've never asked. Of course, it's true that the business world has its own value system . . . But everyone in it knows the score. As it happens, I rarely need to tread on toes. I usually take over companies when they're doing badly and threatening to fold. I get them cheap and I put them back on their feet. It's my speciality.

Sure, there are sometimes people who don't like what I'm doing. But usually they're very grateful to be saved from bankruptcy. I don't *need* to specialise in telling lies for the sort of trading I do.'

'Garston's is profitable,' muttered Jane accusingly, waving aside the desire to believe implicitly every word he said.

'I told you. I'm not planning a take-over at present.'

'You *have* been buying shares, though?'

'Yes.'

'Well!'

'Well nothing. I don't have enough to have a controlling interest. At present I'm no more than a shareholder.'

'A fairly major one, I've no doubt,' she returned scathingly.

'Yes.'

'So it's only a question of time?'

He shook his head. 'Jane, can you just take my word for it that I'm not going to go on buying at present?'

'Why should I?'

'Because this is a very good restaurant and I want us to enjoy our meal.'

She folded her arms defiantly. 'I don't feel like eating,' she said with a scowl.

And then he reached into his jacket pocket and brought out a navy leather box. 'Then if not for the sake of the food, for this...' he said curtly, laying the box on the table and opening it. Inside was a beautiful diamond solitaire. He pushed it towards her.

'What's that?' she asked, aghast, though it was perfectly obvious what it was.

'It's an engagement ring. Yours. I've brought you out tonight to ask you to marry me.'

Jane's lips blanched with shock. She sat very still, staring stupefied at the ring, her brow furrowed into a bewildered frown.

'That's just crazy...' she said, at last.

'I happen to think it's a very good idea.'

Jane let out a weak laugh of disbelief. 'But you don't know me.'

'And *you* most certainly do not know me,' he agreed.

'Then why on earth do you want to marry me? You can't. It doesn't make sense.'

'Doesn't it?'

She shook her head vigorously. 'Of course not!' she cried scornfully. 'You're supposed to love the person you marry. You're supposed to be good friends with them and like them more than anyone else in the whole wide world, and want to share your innermost secrets with them and be with them for every moment of the rest of your life.'

He leaned back in his chair and folded his arms, looking directly into her eyes. A sardonic smile played around the corners of his mouth. 'I guess we could work on all that. But I'll admit we have a way to go yet.'

'You mean you want to go on... go on *courting* me and if all that stuff comes true we'll get engaged?' she queried doubtfully.

'No. I want to marry you. Very soon.'

She found herself looking from side to side as if seeking an escape. This was like a particularly peculiar dream. She shook her head and said nothing. It was horribly bizarre.

She looked across at him. He was watching her carefully. There was no trace of anxiety in his eyes. He did not look like a man who had just asked the most important question of his life and was waiting for his answer. He looked like an astute businessman, laying out a daring proposition before his accountants, and intrigued by the response. What game was he playing with her now? Suddenly she brought one hand up and covered her eyes. Her lower lip was quivering and her chin was puckering ominously.

'I know I'm only twenty-one,' she said in a voice clogged with gathering tears, 'and I must seem very young and foolish to you. And I know I must have sounded ridiculous in that car park, shouting at you about the firm. But this is just cruel. I didn't know that such cruelty existed...' And then big, hot tears began to spill down her face.

'Jane,' he said softly, 'don't cry. Try not to get too emotional. Look at this dispassionately.'

She sniffed hard, and swallowed back a sob. 'Try not to get too emotional?' she echoed incredulously. 'You ask me to marry you in the most cold-blooded manner imaginable, and you don't think it's something to get emotional about?'

His hand came across the table and covered hers. She snatched hers away, and nursed it to her as if scalded.

'I agree that it's all very cold-blooded. But I mean the question seriously, you know? It's not a nasty trick designed to make you feel bad. I really do want you to marry me.'

'Why?'

He handed her a freshly laundered handkerchief. 'Here. Blow your nose. You'll feel better. And let me at least order us an aperitif.'

'So now you want to get me drunk? You've got your seduction routine back to front, Guy. You're supposed to get the lady pie-eyed before you pop the question, not after.'

Guy gave a low chuckle. Damn him. There he was, being human again. Astute, assertive, self-controlled and way, way beyond her comprehension. She could tell that he really did want to marry her for what he considered to be very good reasons, but she was far to naïve to even guess what those reasons might be. She buried her face in the square of fine white linen while he beckoned over the wine waiter and ordered them a dry martini apiece.

'It'll cheer you up. And give you an appetite,' he promised, as she folded the mascara-smudged hanky.

'I couldn't possibly eat a meal with you after that,' she sighed heavily. 'Do I look a mess? Have I got eye make-up all over my face?'

He shook his head. 'The handkerchief took the brunt. You look very beautiful even with red eyes, as it happens.'

The disgust must have shown in her eyes, because he pulled a wry face and added, 'At least you know I'm not lying when I tell you you're beautiful, don't you?'

She gave him a withering, if rather shaky look. 'I'm afraid I've been flattered too often about my appearance to be susceptible on that score. Anyway, I didn't ask you whether I was beautiful. Simply whether I looked a mess.'

'You look fine,' he said reassuringly.

'Take me home,' she said tiredly, as the martinis arrived.

'Drink that first,' he said.

She shook her head. 'What for?'

'Because I want you to give me an hour or so of your company before you give me your answer. I want you to understand why I think we'll be good together. I want you just to relax and enjoy yourself for a couple of hours.'

She eyed him coldly, then picked up the glass and drained it swiftly, gasping as the fierce liquid bit at her throat. She coughed a little then said. 'OK. I've drunk it. I don't feel any different. I still don't want to eat with you—or relax and enjoy your company. And I can't believe you don't already know what my answer is. Now take me home.'

Guy leaned back in his chair and smiled. Then he picked up his own glass and downed it in one.

Jane got to her feet. 'Right,' she said heavily. 'Time to go.'

But Guy remained sitting where he was. 'Sorry,' he said coolly. 'I daren't drive after drinking that on an empty stomach. I was planning to sip it slowly while I ate a hearty meal—an entirely different proposition.'

Jane glowered at him, and then slumped reluctantly back into her chair. She only had a couple of pounds in cash on her, and had neither cheque-book nor credit cards in her slender evening purse. She was a long way from home. She doubted very much she could persuade a taxi driver to take her all the way without showing him the colour of her money first.

Minutes ticked by. She was going to have to stay. She cupped her chin in her hands and sat very still. At last she said, 'I'll have melon to start—that doesn't need cooking, so it shouldn't take long. And salmon in aspic with a green salad and potatoes lyonnaise—that should be quick too. I'd advise you to have the same.'

Guy smiled, and then summoned the waiter to take his order. He studied the menu again at length and then ordered chicken en croute with stilton and roast walnuts. Undoubtedly in a place like this they would cook it from scratch. It was bound to take ages.

CHAPTER FIVE

JANE sat in silence, eyeing Guy sourly for a while before looking away. The trouble was, the sight of him, far from fuelling her disgust, was dissolving it in honey. He was so good to look at. He was relaxed in his chair, his eyes hooded, half watching her watch him, half veiled with contemplation. He was smiling a little, too, his strong white teeth dimly apparent behind his parted lips, and hinting almost provocatively at the moist, dark interior of the mouth beyond.

At last he moved. He brought one tanned, broad hand towards her face, and drew the edge of his thumb from her temple down to her jaw. The seductive gentleness of his touch startled her badly. She clapped her own neatly made hands to her cheeks, and brushed his fingers away.

'Don't do that,' she bit out.

He gave her a reassuring smile. 'Jane, you can sit here and fume all evening if you want. It's up to you. And then you can go home and refuse ever to see me again. It would, of course, be a pointless vanity, but none the less it's an option you are perfectly at liberty to exercise.'

'A *vanity*?'

'Yes. Your pride has been stung tonight. You wouldn't have objected to my proposing marriage at all if only I'd wined and dined you a sufficient number of times, and kissed you on the requisite number of occasions, and asked for your hand in the appropriate manner—preferably alone, by moonlight and beside a lake.'

'You are *so* arrogant!'

'Ah, but I'm not. You see, I'm not suggesting that you necessarily would have accepted me. Merely that you would not have found my request offensive under those circumstances. But I've chosen to do this, as I do most other things, in my own way. Nevertheless, it is a perfectly serious suggestion, and one which I think you'd be a fool to dismiss out of hand simply because your pride has been dented. There'll be ample opportunity for all the wining and dining you could ever want—after we're married.'

She glowered at the tablecloth. 'You're assuming that I'd have *let* you wine and dine and kiss me the requisite number of times...' she returned stiffly.

'You would have,' he said calmly. 'You know perfectly well that you would have. After all, you came tonight, didn't you? My interest in Garston's is the only real objection you've voiced so far.'

Her dark eyes darted up to meet his. 'I've just accused you of arrogance. And...and I remember complaining once that you seemed to know everything without being told. Don't *those* objections count?'

He laughed, a slow, resonant laugh. 'Not at all,' he said, narrowing his slaty blue eyes. 'Those are merely observations—not objections. And I'm quite ready to concede that I'm not perfect. Who in this world is?'

Jane gave a baffled sigh. He certainly didn't think that *she* was. 'I still don't understand why you even made the suggestion. I mean you don't even know me, so you can't possibly be in love with me or anything.'

'I know a lot more about you than you might think,' he countered acidly.

'You're not trying to tell me that you *are* in love with me after all?' she returned, wide-eyed and scornful.

He paused briefly. 'No. Not that,' he said flatly. 'But I do think we could be very, very good together. We can each give exactly what the other needs. I'm very wealthy.

You're very beautiful, and quite capable of handling the sort of life I'm offering with a degree of panache. So just think about it, Jane...'

She shook her head despairingly. 'I can't even *think* about it,' she said honestly. 'I'm just not...not cold-blooded enough for that.'

He studied her for a while longer, watching her unfold her napkin and embark upon her melon. She would get through the meal as best she could because she had no choice. But all she really wanted to do was to go home and close her own bedroom door, and stay there for as long as it took to get this man out of her system. If she could stand spending years on end in her bedroom, that was.

'Jane,' he said firmly at last, and that note was back in his voice—the one which made a physical entity of sound itself. 'You don't know enough about me. You *must* ask me a few questions about myself.'

'I can't,' she confessed warily. 'It would feel like giving in. As if I were taking the idea seriously, and I just can't do that.'

There was another pause and then he smiled wryly, and folded his arms high across his chest. 'I'm glad you asked that,' he said cheerfully. 'Around Sunderland actually—though it's called Tyne and Wear these days.'

She frowned at him, but he just kept smiling. So he was from Sunderland? There was a Lowry painting which swam into her mind...cranes...shipyards...Victorian terraces straggling under grey skies...

He began to speak again, exactly as if she had asked a question and he was replying. 'No. I'm an only child, too, as it happens. Actually, my mother died when I was five.'

Jane fixed her eyes furiously on the melon skin. She scraped at it with her fork. No wonder he hadn't had proper family Christmases.

'Yes, it *was* sad—but not as bad as you might think. I scarcely remembered her, you see. And anyway, she'd been sick for over two years, so she'd become almost shadowy to me even when she was still alive. My father was the one who raised me.'

Without thinking she found herself asking, 'Is he still alive?' She slammed her hand over her mouth.

His smile reached his eyes, but as it did so it died on his lips. 'No, Jane. He died a couple of years ago.' He swallowed hard and she saw his Adam's apple move in his throat and the pupils in his eyes contracted so that they were suddenly very grey and still. Guy had obviously cared very much for his father.

Jane's mouth opened and then closed again. 'I'm sorry,' she said, as a surge of genuine emotion tugged at her. 'Trust me to go and ask the one question which...which...'

He reached out his hand and tweaked the end of her nose, as if she were a child. 'It's OK. You weren't to know. I'll tell you about him, shall I?'

'OK...' she acceded in a small voice.

'Well, he was a machine tool fitter by trade, but his real love was the shed at the bottom of the garden where he made absolutely perfect scale models of steam-engines and rolling-stock. He used to go straight there after work, and would stay there under very late at night.'

She nodded cautiously. So what happened to Guy while his father was in the shed? Was he left all alone?

'...And he used to have track running all around the house—inside and out. He used to deliver messages to me on the trains. He even made a replica post office sorting van for the purpose. I was woken up every morning by a steam train bursting in through a fake tunnel set in my bedroom door and blowing its whistle. Beats the average alarm-clock, eh?'

So he didn't even speak to his son? Simply wrote
messages and sent trains to wake him in the morning?
She found that she was tucking into her salmon without
even being aware of its arrival on the table.

By the time the sweet-trolley arrived her mind was
buzzing with images of trains. There had been a cable-
car overhanging the staircase, the papier mâché mountains concealing the banisters. There had been a London
Underground network beneath the floorboards, emerging
through the bathroom skirting-board to deliver soap—
until someone from the council had come along and put
a stop to it, pointing out that they were contravening
building regulations.

He talked with such an engaging fluency that she could
not help listening. And all the while her mind flashed
back and forth between the images he created of his
childhood, and the memories of her own. She felt hurt
on his behalf. No wonder he was so self-contained . . . so
cool. She'd had all the love in the world. He'd had
scarcely enough to get by. She yearned to ask him about
all the things he didn't mention—his friendships, his
frustrations, his feelings. But she dared not. It would
imply an intimacy . . . an intimacy which he, despite his
proposal of marriage, clearly didn't want. No wonder
he had chosen to do this thing in his own way. Everybody
else's way—the moonlight and roses way—was shuttered
and barred to him. He had never been invited into that
world.

She tried to visualise him as a boy, eating Sunday lunch
alone with his father, but she couldn't make the mental
picture jell. She sighed heavily. The small box still sat
on the table between them. It was closed, but she could
picture the ring inside very clearly indeed.

At last the meal was finished and the ordeal nearly
over. As they went back out to the car she suddenly

turned and looked up at him. 'How old are you?' she
asked.

'Thirty-four.'

'And you've never been married?'

'No. But I haven't been celibate, either.'

She shrugged. 'I didn't suppose you had,' she said
softly. That wasn't what she'd wanted to know. She'd
wanted to know whether he'd ever been in love—but she
didn't have the nerve to ask.

The sky above prickled with stars.

'I shan't marry you, you know...' she said, but even
as she said it something tired and heavy, almost like a
keening, sounded a discordant note in her head. What
was the matter with her? She didn't *want* to marry him,
did she? She opened her hands helplessly. 'I don't
understand any of this,' she sighed. 'Why did you buy
the shares, for instance?'

He didn't answer for a moment. Then he said, 'If you
marry me, they will be your wedding present.' And his
eyes narrowed, obsidian in the darkness, withdrawn and
austere.

Jane frowned. 'But you started buying ages ago.'

'After I kissed you, as it happens,' he said neutrally.

Jane gulped. 'Do you mean that's when you decided?
When you kissed me?'

'That's not when I decided to ask you to marry me.
But I could tell from the kiss that we'd be good in bed
together,' he replied levelly. 'It was very obvious.'

Her skin burned at his directness. 'Is that why...?'
she stuttered. 'I mean...just because I'm...well,
attractive.'

'No.' There was something undeniably honest about
his response. 'If it were simply your body that I wanted,
Jane, I'd have had it by now.'

And then, without touching her with his hands, he
lowered his mouth and let his dry, parted lips brush

across hers, side to side, very gently. She was taken aback by the gesture. She hadn't expected him to kiss her this evening. He had made his offer in too business-like a way for her to imagine that he would use passion as a tactic. And anyway, only seconds earlier he'd said...? He'd said...? But she couldn't work it out. Not now while his mouth was moving against hers like that. She could smell the maleness of him. It assaulted the very air she breathed, making it catch in her throat as she dragged it into her lungs. His lips travelled over her face, still feather-light, fragile, haunting. His breath fanned across her hot skin, making desire rush and rattle rhythmically inside her like a speeding train. She pressed her dry lips together and stood very still.

Would he kiss her properly again? Surely he would...? To remind her...to tempt her... She shook with anticipation and waited, quite unable to steel herself to resist. His mouth reached her neck, nibbling and butting softly at the tender skin behind her ears. With a surprising delicacy she felt the hot tip of his tongue lick the lobe of her ear. He raised one hand then, and she was sure he would take her by the shoulder and pull her to him, but he simply curled his fingers around the silky mass of her hair and lifted it up and away from her nape. When his mouth reached the hard bump of her vertebrae created by the submissive droop of her head, his lips parted wide and the moist fullness of his mouth pressed hard against her skin. His teeth bit into her skin as his tongue found the prominence and caressed it roughly. Jane's entire body seemed to be weakening and melting at the promise of what was to come. She could hardly breathe.

And then his mouth freed her and his hand let her hair drop. She felt a few strands stick to the damp circle of skin he had left behind. She waited for him to come and face her and begin to kiss her properly. But it didn't happen.

Instead he took a few paces away from her towards the car. The back of her neck seemed suddenly very cold.

'Why did you do that?' she asked, her quaking voice betraying her arousal.

He made an abrupt, disdainful noise in the back of his throat. 'To prove my point.' And he opened the car door and got behind the wheel.

She felt horribly ashamed of herself. She joined him in the car, letting her hair fall forward to shield her face. Was he right? If he'd made a play for her body, would she have given in?

Oh, what was the matter with her? She knocked her clenched knuckles rapidly against each other, as if fighting herself. How could she have been so eager for him to kiss her after everything he'd said? She'd been mesmerised from the moment his mouth touched hers. She made her hands relax and laid them in her lap, watching the patterns of lights shifting and changing beyond the windscreen. The silence in the car shivered between them.

She had to admit to a suspicion that if he'd gone about things differently she might well have let him make love to her—if he'd wined her and dined her and kissed her the requisite number of times, that was. He stirred some great carnal need in her, and she seemed to be powerless in the face of it. Oh, dear. She wasn't going to find herself agreeing to marry him just for the sake of this...this chemistry, was she?

'Couldn't we just have an affair?' she suddenly blurted out, one hand tightening around the other wrist as she spoke.

'No,' he returned expressionlessly.

Her shame swelled and grew until it seemed like a shroud enveloping her. She found herself remembering that silly business over the peanut. He'd thought from the outset that she'd been offering sex. No doubt all her protests had just seemed like a calculated change of tactics—the old game of playing hard to get. And then when he'd kissed her and touched her as if to test her out, she—*fool*—had behaved like a little wanton in his arms... And yet he didn't want an affair? He claimed to want to marry her. Was he calling her bluff? But none of this felt like a bluff at all. It felt coldly, dispassionately real. That sense of shame seared her with renewed force. She *had* to understand. 'Please, just tell me why...' she said with a husky urgency.

'Jane, you can work it out. It's really not that difficult.'

'*Spell* it out...' she insisted.

He sighed for the second time that evening. 'Well, Jane, there's your family background for a start... It counts for a lot as far as I'm concerned. And my age, of course... And then, I have more money than I know what to do with. Houses. Yachts.' He let out another insulting sigh. 'Godammit, Jane Garston—figure it out for yourself. It really isn't difficult.'

For the rest of the journey she did just that. His response had brought relief flooding through her. At least it wasn't all down to the fact that he thought she'd be... good in bed. She hadn't inadvertently brought all this upon herself because she was attracted to him. He wanted to marry her because she came from a... well, from a very old-established family.

Yes. It made a kind of sense. He'd come from a modest background and had made a lot of money, and now he was ready to marry and she was just the right type of wife for him. She could see exactly what he meant now. He'd moved on in the world socially and he needed a wife who would fit in. The kiss had just been a way of ascertaining that the physical side would be OK too.

He'd have needed to satisfy himself on that account, but really the decision was entirely pragmatic.

So he really *had* meant it when he said he had come to court her that first day? Apart from the outstanding business of the kiss, the decision had been all but taken.

'Don't you think that love is important?' she asked quietly.

He shrugged. 'Are you so sure that you think that *you* do? It seems to me that that's the crucial question.'

'I think it matters. I think it's the only thing that does matter.'

'You've got a very conventional idea of love, haven't you?'

'So have most people.'

'But you're not most people, are you, Jane Garston? You don't come from a conventional family background, any more than I do. We've both done very well without convention so far. So are you really so sure that marriage has to be based on fairy-tales in order to work?'

'I *do* come from a conventional family background,' she contradicted.

He shrugged. 'Well, yes... up to a point...'

Oh, dear. She could see it *all* now. Even the fact that she had been adopted from a Brazilian orphanage would count in her favour. It made her less... less 'establishment'. Less likely to cause problems in the years ahead, because she was, in a sense, an outsider too. She could see now why it had to be her and not someone else.

'So the fact that I was born into another culture matters?'

'It's a fact of life. That's all. Of course, it doesn't matter in itself... but perhaps it's had some effect on you, none the less? You must have considered from time to time how different your life would have been if you hadn't been adopted.'

'Naturally.' But she wasn't really speaking the truth.
Fate had taken control of her life. She had never needed
to consider what might have been.

'Perhaps it's made you realise on an unconscious level
that things *can* be done differently?'

'You mean, sort of, arranged marriages? Marriages
where love isn't the overriding motive?'

He was silent. He just kept his eyes on the road ahead.

Of course, he was right. She *had* been born into
another culture. For an orphan in a city like Rio, a proposal from a man like Guy would seem like heaven on
earth. So was her rejection just a vanity, as he had
suggested?

Then she bit her lip angrily. Oh, this was absurd. It
was no good him suggesting that she could do things
differently because she came from another culture...
because she had only ever known one culture, one
family... She wasn't like her school-friend Mumtaz, who
had happily gone into an arranged marriage, knowing
that, for her, real love would grow from respect. Mumtaz
was lucky. She had roots in two cultures—an extra di-
mension to her life which had enabled her to make that
choice.

Jane sighed. 'I wish I hadn't come this evening,' she
said.

He shrugged. 'I'm expecting you to change your mind
about that. Anyway, as I pointed out before, you couldn't
help yourself. You fancy me, Jane, whether you're prepared to admit it or not. Now why don't you put your
time to good use and ask me some more about myself?'

'No...' she wailed insistently. 'I'm not going to marry
you, so why should I do that? Anyway, it's such a cold
way of going about it. If you'd courted me properly it
would have seemed natural—but this...well!'

He made an impatient noise with his mouth. 'Jane—
if I'd done things the conventional way it would have

been dishonest. It might have got me the result I wanted—but I didn't want to trick you into believing that sexual attraction was the same thing as love. Can't you at least see that although this may seem callous, at least it ensures that you know exactly where you stand? If you agree to be my wife now, we can build something really good—without any pretence or disappointment or disillusionment threatening to undermine us. If you married me because you'd fooled yourself into believing that you loved me, things could only go downhill when you finally realised the truth. It would be an appalling waste, and not one I'm prepared to risk.'

'Ye-es . . .' She sighed wearily. 'I can see that. But I'm afraid it doesn't make me feel any better about it.'

And then, all of a sudden, in her mind's eye, she *could* see him as a small boy, eating Sunday lunch with his father. A cold lunch served by a cold man who wanted to get back to his garden shed and stay there until late at night. A man who never wasted a moment of his precious time on human relationships. He was all Guy had had. And the boy had worshipped him. No wonder Guy was obsessed by his work. No wonder he thought love between man and wife didn't matter.

She glanced across at his profile and swallowed hard. He still seemed remote; but he no longer seemed ruthless in her eyes.

A funny feeling had come to sit in Jane's stomach as all this ran through her mind. It was a heavy, sullen feeling. It was as if she were full of tears—but the tears were solid and cold, like gravel. They weren't capable of being shed. Was this the dull ache of grief which had settled beneath her heart? She laid her cheek against the cold glass of the window beside her and sighed.

If he hadn't been so sure of himself . . . if he'd gone the conventional route and bided his time and taken her to a lakeside by moonlight and behaved like a man who had fallen in love, she might have let him put that diamond solitaire on her finger after all. Because she knew that she didn't just fancy him, now. It seemed she had fallen in love with him. So he was right. She might have fooled herself, and would one day have broken her heart when she realised he didn't love her in return.

She almost ran away from him when they reached the door. 'Don't contact me again,' she pleaded. 'I won't change my mind.'

'You will,' he said softly, and his eyes gleamed in the darkness. 'And I'm sure you'll find a way to get in touch with me when you have.'

She lay awake all night trying to come to terms with the fact that although she now loved him, and wanted him more than anything in the world, she would never, ever allow herself to marry him.

In the morning her mother said, 'You're tired. You have that air about you when you're tired...' She laughed affectionately. 'It was there when you were just a tiny baby, too. All our friends in this country said we were mad—that I should come back home and forget you and adopt a child over here. But I loved you, you see ... and I understood you. No one else would have known when you were tired just by the look in your eyes. I couldn't leave you. For better or worse, it had to be you...'

Fate. It had all been meant to be. Would any other woman ever understand why Guy hid his emotions so carefully? Would any other woman ever love him, knowing that it would take time and tenderness for him to learn to love in return?

Suddenly there didn't seem to be a choice any more. And indeed it wasn't difficult to get hold of the phone number of Rexford Holdings' head office in London. Nor to leave an urgent message for him to contact her at six p.m. At six o'clock and thirty seconds the phone in her room rang.

'Hello? Guy?'

There was a brief pause. Then his voice came crackling drily down the line. 'You're going to agree. Tremendous! I can tell by your voice. You sound frightened to death. It can only mean one thing.'

Jane gave a shaky sigh and rubbed anxiously at one eye. 'Is that how you want your fiancée to sound when she agrees to marry you? Frightened to death?'

He laughed. 'It's only temporary. You'll soon get used to the idea. You'll sound pleased with yourself then.'

'Er...what happens next? Are you coming over to take me out to celebrate, or what?'

'I'm in London on business,' he said briskly. 'I could be with you in a couple of hours, though I'd have to get back... Look, tomorrow's Saturday and——'

Her heart jumped painfully. 'That's OK,' she said with a forced brightness, pressing the receiver hard against one ear, and twisting her gold earring in the other. 'Tomorrow will do fine. But the only thing is, Guy, could we please not say anything to my parents for a week or so? I want them to think you've been wining and dining me as per normal and that you proposed to me by moonlight beside a lake...'

'A couple of weeks? I was hoping we'd be married by then!'

'No...quite soon. But...but not with indecent haste, please. I just want it all to seem very normal to Mum and Dad.'

There was a little silence and then he said, 'OK. Whatever you say. I'll be with you around ten. Dress casually—I'll take you for a picnic if the weather holds up.'

CHAPTER SIX

THE wedding took place six weeks later. It was a June wedding, with six bridesmaids and three hundred guests. Very conventional.

Guy had played his part well from the moment the decision was made. He was faultlessly charming, and took her on a two-week round of dinners and parties and nightclubs. Each evening ended chastely, without so much as a brisk peck on the cheek, so that in the end Jane found herself suggesting clubs where they could dance. She adored the sensation of moving with him, his big hands on her back, hers slipped around his waist, beneath his jacket, fingering the silky back of his waistcoat covertly as they swayed to the music, and allowing herself to indulge the heady glow of being close to the man she loved.

But once the engagement had been announced Jane hardly saw Guy. His work took him to Malaysia and India, and seemed to require his presence in London an awful lot of the time. Jane made the effort to understand his need to distance himself.

Jane's mother cried at the wedding. Big salty tears rearranged her make-up. Jane's father did, too. Tears of joy stood sentinel in his gentle grey eyes, but manfully declined to course down his cheeks. Jane didn't cry. She stood proudly at the altar, her chin high, looking more beautiful than any bride had a right to look. This too, she told herself as the wide gold band was slipped on to her finger, is meant to be. And when she looked up at her groom as he lifted her veil, and lowered his mouth very slowly to kiss her, her heart filled to bursting with love and she sent up an earnest prayer. *Please, God. Oh, please let it all work out.*

After the reception a chauffeur-driven Rolls took them to London and deposited them at an exclusive hotel.

'You look exhausted,' he said as she perched nervously on the edge of the sofa in their suite. It wasn't, she noticed, the honeymoon suite. It wasn't even decked with flowers. A small bowl of freesias sat on the coffee-table in front of her, filling the room with their fragrance. It was very nice, but not the least bit bridal. It was exactly what she ought to have expected, if only she'd stopped to think. She'd been too carried away with the wedding preparations, that was the trouble.

'I am tired,' she admitted, taking off the small, turquoise velvet hat which matched the silk suit she had worn to come away. 'It's been a long day. A long six weeks, come to that...'

'You don't regret it?' he asked directly, fixing her with his eyes.

'No.'

'So you discovered that love doesn't matter that much, after all?'

Jane looked away, fixing her eyes very hard on a patch of wallpaper on the other side of the room. 'No, Guy. I didn't discover *quite* that. It was the love of my parents which made up my mind for me in the end.'

'You mean you married me solely for their sake? For the shares?'

'No.' Jane shook her head vehemently. She couldn't bear him to think she'd married him for money. 'Not that. More for the fact that they want so much for me...they love me so dearly...they want me to have...' She was about to say happiness, but caught herself back. She didn't want to give away the fact that she was in love with him yet. Not until he was ready to love her too... 'Everything,' she substituted lamely. Then added more emphatically, 'Everything in abundance.'

'I see,' he said, and he slowly began to loosen his tie. 'Let's hope that they get their hearts' desire then,' he added laconically.

Jane felt embarrassed. This wasn't a very appropriate conversation to be having on their wedding night. She flashed him a weak, eager little smile. 'What shall we do this evening?' she asked, and then flinched, realising that that hadn't exactly been the right thing to say, either.

'What do you want to do?' he asked wearily. 'More wining and dining and dancing?'

'No,' she muttered morosely. Oh, wasn't it obvious what she wanted him to do? 'Not that. Not tonight.'

'It's nine o'clock,' he said glancing at his watch, and stretching out in the chair opposite her. 'Perhaps if we have a meal sent up shortly we can manage an early night. We'll have to get going first thing in the morning.' He picked up the remote control for the TV set and switched it on.

Jane's eyes widened with dismay. 'Uh... yes.' So was this to be her wedding night, then? Eating off a tray while they watched TV?

She looked away from Guy. For six weeks the idea of this night had curled inside her mind, like a contented cat licking cream from its whiskers. She had tried to push the thought away, because that *wasn't* why she was marrying him. Yet still the image had come, unbidden, of them together on their wedding night, bedded in white linen, arms entwined...

She swallowed hard. 'Where are we going for our honeymoon? Can I know now?'

'Tuscany. I have a home there. It's nice. You'll like it. I thought we could live there for a while. I can commute quite easily.'

'Oh...' So there wasn't even to be a proper honeymoon? And then sharp tears brightened her big, dark eyes and she blinked and blinked but they wouldn't go away, and in the end she had to get hastily to her feet and find the bathroom and blow her nose.

When she came back into the room he said, 'You're disappointed, aren't you?'

'Why should I be? Tuscany's lovely.' She scoured her mind for something bright and positive to say. The paintings, of course... every church for miles around had the most splendid paintings... and the Uffizi gallery... 'We'll be within striking distance of Florence. It's one of my favourite cities,' she added with a firm smile. 'It's a wonderful place.'

He was in the middle of shrugging off his jacket. 'It's certainly very smart. Lots of boutiques and good restaurants.'

Although his face betrayed nothing, that edge was back in his voice, and she felt abraded by it. She let her eyes settle on the television screen. Anything rather than look at his waistcoat, superbly fitted over his broad chest... And his long legs stretched out in front of him... And his head tilted at an angle so that his jaw stuck out in bold relief over his loosened shirt-collar.

Oh, lord... only a couple of hours and she would see him undressed for the first time and he would take her in his arms, and it wouldn't matter that he hadn't bothered with any of the romantic trappings because... because she did love him very, very much and even thinking about it was making her burn with desire. She wriggled in her seat.

'Hungry?' he asked.

His eyes met hers. Inky. She looked deeply into them. 'Yes...' she said.

'I'll call room service.'

She smiled her agreement. They would eat together alone for the first time, and then relax together alone for the first time. And then they would make love. Together. For the first time.

But he didn't make love with her that night. She bathed luxuriously in scented water and put on her flimsy white silk nightgown, and she let down her swathe of black, shiny hair and walked nervously into their bedroom. He was standing next to the bed, wearing just a pair of navy briefs. She almost cried aloud at this first sight of him without his business suit or the crisp, designer casuals he wore for informal occasions. He was so unutterably beautiful. His skin was taut and brown, stretched over packed muscle and bone. Dark hairs curled crisply against the skin of his chest, and tapered beckoningly beneath his navel. He was hard and powerful and muscular and very, very male. The muscles of his thighs tightened and then relaxed as she came into the room. And then he looked at her very seriously, and he took her arm and led her to the bed and she thought... oh...good grief...it was happening and she could hardly think at all.

His hand began by fondling the back of her neck.

'You're worn out.'

'Oh, not really...' she denied earnestly, praying that the question of an early night had been buried for good. 'It's been a lovely day...really wonderful. It was a super wedding wasn't it? It's left me feeling very...wide awake. Very...ready for anything.'

His hands shooed her hair over her shoulders and plied the muscles of her neck.

'Lie on your stomach...' he said.

When she complied he began to massage her back. It was glorious... Any minute now he would turn her over and his mouth would cover hers and they would kiss. But it didn't happen. Her desire mounted until she was gasping and moaning, her fingers digging into the yielding banks of pillows. And, although her face was pressed against the starched pillow-slip and she could see nothing, she could feel the hard strength of his arousal matching her own, and could hear his breathing falter and the sounds of his mouth swallowing convulsively against the force of carnal need. Soon. It must be soon, surely? But just as she felt that neither of them could bear this restraint any longer he let his hands drift away from her skin.

'Sleep now,' he said thickly, and he rolled away from her and lay on his side with his back to her.

'Aren't you going to make love with me?' she asked, muffled, her teeth against the pillow.

'Not now. It'll be better if we wait...' he said, and she bit very, very hard on her lower lip and waited for the pangs to subside. They were tired. Both of them. And there was no reason why, in their case, they should follow tradition to the letter. He was very experienced, after all, while she was very much a virgin. Wasn't he always right? But when at last she heard his breathing fall into the steady rhythm of sleep she wept.

He was already dressed in a pair of smoky blue chinos and a grey chambray shirt when she woke up. His chin shone from the assault of the razor and his hair was damp from the shower. Even such soft, casual clothes looked fresh and new-made on his big, square frame. Jane dressed in the bathroom. Taking her lead from him, she put on an undemanding madras sundress in russet and blue checks, with a baggy matching jacket and flat sandals. She left her hair loose.

'I'll get them to take our bags down before we have breakfast,' he said. 'Is there anything you want from the suitcase?'

'I don't know. I don't know what we'll be doing today...' she returned vaguely.

'Helicopter and then private jet to Pisa,' he returned crisply. 'I'll drive us the rest of the way. We should be there for lunch.'

The narrow roadway to the house was composed of pale stones and faded dust. It wound, dry, yellow, mysterious, between an avenue of cypress trees. Beyond the trees were well tended vineyards. At the road's vanishing point shimmered an ethereal blue vision of misty mountains. The house was set off to one side, hidden by the dark plumes of the trees until they were almost upon it. It was white. Its windows, viewed across the sun-washed garden, seemed too small for its wide expanse. The orange pantiles of the roof looked bleached and dry under the brash midday sun.

'What a pretty road. It's like something in a dream,' said Jane, looking straight ahead at the mountains. She was afraid to comment on the house—or to look at it more than was necessary. She no longer felt certain that all this was meant to be. She was frightened.

'It's hell in winter. It just turns to mud,' said Guy, swinging the well-sprung cabriolet on to the tarmacked driveway. 'We'll live in a city in winter, of course. London. Paris. New York. You can choose.' He brought the car round in front of the house. 'What do you think?'

She forced herself to look again at the house. It had two turrets with conical tiled roofs. 'It's beautiful,' she said truthfully, unable to fault the confection in front of her. Now that they were nearer, the windows looked larger. She could see a mosaic-floored porch, blue and white and yellow, framing an arched doorway.

'There are a couple of pools at the back,' elaborated Guy, silencing the car and getting out. He stretched and yawned before coming around to her side and opening the door. 'I've got two local women coming in most mornings to do the work, but otherwise we'll have the place to ourselves.'

'Oh.' Jane felt less fearful all of a sudden. There was something magical about this house. She was sure that being alone with him here would be better than any honeymoon she could have dreamt up.

Inside was all cool white marble and more mosaic tiles. The hallway was bare of furniture, but there was a small painting on the wall of a peasant-woman with a basket on her hip.

She reached down and unhooked the backs of her sandals from her heels and stood barefoot on the cold floor, her shoes dangling from one hand, her eyes transfixed by the picture. 'It's a Pissarro, isn't it?' she said wonderingly. It was so good . . . so wholesome and animated and *nourishing*. She wriggled her toes excitedly.

Guy came up behind her. 'How did you know?'

'I did an art appreciation class,' she said drily. 'And I got the bug then. Especially for the Impressionists.' The lessons had bred in her a genuine love of painting. 'It *is* a Pissarro, isn't it?'

He laid his hands on her bare shoulders and looked at the painting with her. 'Yes,' was all he said, but she felt his approval sweep over her. Without being conscious of what she was doing, she leant back against him. His fingers began to move gently against her skin. She closed her eyes briefly. Now, she willed. Take me upstairs and make love with me now. They stood there like that for some minutes. She could feel his heart pounding and his breath warm in her hair. And she could sense a tightening of his muscles, a hardening of flesh as her weight tended against his and her breasts began to firm themselves into demanding points.

And then he took a step backwards. 'It's a nice picture, isn't it?' he asked.

She quelled the pangs of disappointment. 'Mmmm,' she managed. Then she ran a finger along the edge of her sundress. 'I'm awfully hot,' she said as steadily as she could.

'Go upstairs and explore,' he said. 'You can take a shower. I'll bring the cases up. You can slip into a swimsuit then and we'll have lunch by the pool.'

And that was exactly what did happen, though while she was in the shower she heard him moving about the adjoining bedroom and was certain that he must come in and find her drenching herself in the lukewarm spray, her senses expectant, her eyes shining, and *then* he would begin to kiss her. But the sounds died, and when she walked naked into the bedroom it was to find his clothes folded carefully over the back of a simple wooden chair, but the man himself quite absent.

She picked out a bikini without thinking. She didn't know quite what made her fingers travel to that particular swimsuit because she had several. But once she had secured its fastenings she knew exactly why she had chosen it. It was a luscious, deep raspberry pink, and the top scarcely covered the full, round orbs of her golden breasts. She had to be careful as she tied the skinny neckstraps not to touch her breasts, because by now her flesh was practically crying out with desire. She looked over her shoulder in the mirror as she tied up her hair and saw the curves of her her hips laid bare by the enticingly skimpy briefs. It was a very provocative bikini indeed.

Guy was already in the pool, which was screened from the house by more cypress trees. She walked nervously to the edge of the sparkling blue water, raised her arms, paused for a moment to make sure his eyes were following her and executed a competent dive. She surfaced close to him. He was standing chest deep in the water, his pupils made small by the sunlight, his skin wet and gleaming. His eyes narrowed as they watched her. His black, dense eyelashes were full of water.

'You dive well,' he said.

'Not really. I can only do a swallow-dive from the edge. I can't dive off boards or anything.'

He nodded into the distance. 'There's a diving pool at the end of that path. You can practise——'

'Guy!' The noise was somewhere between a plea and a wail.

He gave a small, dry smile, his eyes starting to rake over her wet shoulder. 'What's the matter?'

'I *don't* want to talk about diving,' she said shakily.

'Oh...?'

'No,' she continued despairingly. 'I want to know why you didn't...um... The thing is, Guy, you said we'd be good in bed together, so although we haven't married for all the usual reasons I didn't suppose it would be a...you know, a celibate sort of a marriage...' She tailed off weakly.

'Last night, when I massaged your back—did that feel celibate?'

'Well, no. But even so...'

'I still fancy you, Jane Rexford,' he said drily.

Jane touched the edge of the pool, hung on and sighed. 'Then why don't you want to make love with me, Guy?' she found herself asking bitterly. 'Isn't this going to be a real marriage after all? I don't understand. I thought that although we'd married for our own reasons, the marriage itself would be just like anyone else's. Not an...empty shell.'

He lifted a hand from the water and stroked her cheek with his damp fingertips.

'I want to make love to you very badly indeed,' he said, his voice low. 'I would have thought that was obvious.'

'Then why don't you? We *are* married!'

'Because,' he said, letting his hand come to rest on her shoulder, and then letting it travel below the surface until it brushed against the hard point of one breast, 'because there needs to be a period first in which I discover what will please you. Everyone is different, Jane...'

'A period of courtship, you mean?' she asked challengingly. Suddenly she was angry with him. 'You said when you took me to lunch that first time that you had come to court me. And then you just...stopped. But it's six weeks since I agreed to marry you, and you've had plenty of time since then to court me. Why did you leave it so late?'

He smiled, and the sunlight on the strong planes of his face made her ache inside. 'I've already courted you,' he said. 'I've courted you and I've wed you. But I still have to woo you, Jane.'

'Then you've had six weeks in which to woo me!'

'Jane, you're young—and a virgin. Trust me. It will be better this way. You'll see...' And then he kissed her wet mouth very passionately and let his fingers explore the taut thrust of her breasts through the scant bikini top. At last, when she was finding it hard to catch her breath, and her knees started buckling so that she kept sinking in the water, he stopped, and let go of her and swam powerfully to the edge of the pool. As he heaved himself out, his desire for her was indeed very obvious. She felt herself colour deeply, but didn't follow him. Already she felt she had let herself down by almost pleading with him to consummate their marriage quickly. This wasn't a normal marriage, she reminded herself. He, at least, wasn't overwhelmed by love and desperate to have it made manifest. She was, of course. But it wouldn't do to have him guess.

She stayed in the water a little longer in the hope that her desire would fade, but when she saw him stand up and stretch so that his hard abdomen hollowed and all the hairs on his thighs prickled up into a dark fuzz she realised that viewing him from a distance was no better than seeing him close to. She reluctantly pulled herself out of the water and joined him on a rug nearby, where food spilled out of a hamper and a Chianti bottle stood uncorked.

They ate tomatoes and cheese, thinly sliced cold meats, fresh bread, peaches and cherries, all the while lying side by side on the rug.

Guy let his hands travel lightly over her bare stomach as she ate, and murmured, 'This is going to be wonderful. You'll see. You won't be sorry in the end that I've made you wait.'

She propped her head on one hand and looked into his dark eyes. 'I know. I'm sure you're right. I shouldn't have been so impatient.'

But Guy was not listening to her words. His eyes had been captured by the fall of her breasts as she stretched out on her side, and slowly, using his teeth to tug away her bikini top, he let his mouth hover hungrily over her breasts before letting his tongue circle the dark peaks of her exposed nipples. The sensation startled her with its power to arouse. The need she had felt so far had been a diffuse, gentle thing compared to this. Now pleasure attacked her senses like lemon juice on the tongue. She lay back in the sun and closed her eyes, while her breasts taught her how sharp and demanding her arousal could be. She lay like that for what seemed like a long time, letting the insistent pulse of her need beat its tattoo in time to the motion of his mouth on her breasts. When he dragged hard against her nipples with his teeth she shuddered and squirmed her shoulder-blades against the rug.

He stopped. 'Did you like that a lot, or didn't you like it at all?' he asked with a detatchment which was belied only by the rough burr of his voice.

'I...I don't know,' she admitted. 'I...it was a strange sensation. I think I could like it...I'm sure I ought to but——'

'Jane, there are no *oughts* in lovemaking,' he said. 'That why I wanted us to wait. To take our time. There is only what gives us both pleasure. I shan't do that again until we're more certain of each other, and I'm sure that you're confident enough to tell me to stop if you want me to. If you're not convinced that you like something another time you must tell me.'

He stared forbiddingly down into her big, dark brown eyes. She looked up at him for a long time without speaking. He had been right. She wouldn't have made any comment about what she did or didn't enjoy, left to her own devices. Putting her trust in him, she whispered, 'I liked it when you teased me with your tongue...and when you know, when you...um...um...' She used her hand to show him what she meant.

He smiled at her very tenderly then. 'Good. We're married to one another, Jane. Man and wife together. We have all the time in the world to learn all sorts of things...but for the moment we'll stick with what we already know.'

He didn't drag his teeth across her skin the next time. And the pleasure he gave her became increasingly unmarred by uncertainty. All through the long afternoon he kissed her and touched her. When her need became too intense to bear she would utter a sharp cry, and he would stop. Occasionally he stopped anyway, his breathing hard and forced and the muscles of his jaw clenched, and she sensed that he too was finding it very difficult to control his desire.

At last, when the afternoon had filtered away, Guy said, 'Come on...let's swim again. Then we can get a meal.'

Jane sat up and groaned. 'Guy... this afternoon has been the most wonderful lesson in the art of arousal I could possibly imagine. But I feel as if I'm going to burst with it all. I can't just stop and swim and cook a meal as if I'd been reading the newspaper all afternoon. Don't you see?'

Guy knelt beside her and tipped back his head. He smiled very broadly, his eyes narrowing and his lips parting to show his even white teeth. He laughed. It was a happy sound. 'You see... I was right. You're not shy, now. You're beginning to feel OK talking about it.'

'Don't you think that would have happened anyway?' she complained.

He shrugged. 'I don't believe in leaving things to chance,' he said firmly and then stood up, loped across to the pool and dived in.

She sighed. If they'd both been in love she was sure there would have been no inhibitions... after all, that was what shared love meant, didn't it? But they *weren't* both in love... so this was the way it had to be... She stretched out her heavy, languorous limbs and arched her spine. Then slowly she got to her feet and walked across to the pool, plopping herself gently into the water, watching while Guy swam powerfully from one end to the other. She took a few tentative strokes. She was so hot that at least the coolness of the water against her skin was good. She headed for the opposite end, swimming slowly but steadily. Guy was up ahead, turning to complete another length, the water around him foaming with turbulence, the muscles of his brown shoulders outlined against the white spray.

She closed her eyes and increased her speed, concentrating on getting across the pool as fast as possible. When she arrived at the far end she turned and swam the next length even faster. She had never paced herself when she swam before, but suddenly she was fixing her eyes on the expanse of blue water ahead of her and willing it to part for her. Her arms ached from the effort. Was this what drove people onwards in life? Disappointment? Rejection? Frustration? She glanced across at Guy, ploughing through the water almost ferociously. Was that what had driven him all his life?

By the time they were ready to come out of the water both of them had driven their sexual needs into abeyance with physical effort.

Guy put one hand on her shoulder as they walked, barefoot, back through the garden to the house, and the sensation of wet skin on her tired flesh hardly stirred her at all.

'Look,' he said, indicating the back of the house. 'It's a sort of U-shape. It means that the courtyard is always well-shaded, no matter what time of day it is. We'll eat out there, I think.'

Jane nodded. 'Is there plenty of food in?'

'Yes. I arranged for the fridge to be well-stocked. I didn't think we'd want to go shopping for a few days at least.'

She felt pleased when he said that. It seemed to bode well. 'You're incredibly well-organised,' she said admiringly.

'I need to be,' he agreed. 'I live life at a pretty fast pace.'

'Don't you ever let go and just relax?' she sighed.

And then he caught hold of her chin and turned her face towards his, and said, 'Oh, yes. And you'll find out just how relaxed I can be before long.'

Jane felt her lips part in a smile. 'Before dinner or after?' she teased.

He narrowed his eyes. 'After...' he growled.

She couldn't bear it any more. She leaned against his broad chest and sighed and said, 'No, Guy. Now. Please.'

But he just set her firmly aside and said, 'Later.'

Later, Jane couldn't deny that it had been worth waiting for. He kissed her and caressed her and touched her and teased her. This time there was no stopping. No holding back. Each time his mouth found her mouth or travelled over her shoulders to cover a breast her need mounted even further. At first it spiralled upwards gently, then charged onwards relentlessly, until she abruptly moved into a new realm of arousal. She had entered a world where she was open and moist and ready, driven by an urgency which would not be stayed. Until now Guy had been leading her. Suddenly she felt as if she was travelling alone, driven only by the animal force of her desire. She clung to him, her limbs winding around him, her body arching and pleading with a thousand small movements, her breasts rubbing against the rough hairs of his chest, her teeth feinting at the sleek brown skin of his shoulders, her voice moaning wildly, her skin slick with sweat. And then it happened. With a dark, animal thrust he entered her. There was no pain. Only the sensation of them being made one, racing together towards a glorious light. As he moved inside her all her senses seemed to falter for a moment, and then hurled themselves into a formless ecstasy which left her boneless and shaking, and utterly, utterly happy.

CHAPTER SEVEN

WHEN Jane woke up the next morning, Guy was sprawled on his stomach beside her, his head turned away, still sleeping peacefully. He had slipped down the bed a little, so that he lay flat out on the mattress, his big, well-shaped feet hanging over the end of the bed. Her heart leapt in her throat. He looked so beautiful— and so endearingly vulnerable, his arms flung out carelessly, his shoulders rising and falling with each steady breath. She wanted to hug him close, to hold his head against her naked breasts. But of course she couldn't do that because it would be too intimate and tender a gesture for a relationship such as theirs. Instead she simply looked, noticing another mole close to his spine, and the few stray hairs which peppered his shoulders. Her eyes ran upwards to the hair of his head, shorn close against his powerful neck. It had been cut so short that it was impossible to tell whether it was severely straight or might have curled given a chance. A dark, rich brown, thick and springy; her fingers itched to reach into it and riffle it. She stretched out one hand and touched it.

Guy stirred, and then, still lying on his stomach, turned his head to face her.

Jane's response was to let out a short, horrified scream.

His eyes opened, dark blue and bleary, and then his brow gathered into a frown. 'Jane?' he said in a gravelly, early-morning voice, his face crumpled against the sheet.

'Uh...oh, dear...' Jane's hand was shaking as she pressed it to her mouth and her heart was hammering crazily.

Guy slowly sat up, continuing to look at her and continuing to frown. 'Was I imagining it or did you scream?'

'I screamed...' she admitted, giving a tremulous laugh in confirmation. 'You gave me a horrible fright.'

Guy pulled a bemused face. 'Why? I mean, what did I do?'

'I...Guy, you've got a beard.'

And then it was Guy's turn to laugh, as he reached up a hand to rub raspingly at his chin. 'I'm sorry. I got carried away last night. I should have shaved before I went to bed.'

Jane peered at his dense, black stubble. 'How many times a day do you have to shave it?' she asked.

'Two. Three. It depends.'

She peered even more closely at his chin. 'That's incredible. You've grown proper designer stubble overnight. When any of my friends have tried it, it's taken them a few days, at the very least. Do you drink fertiliser?'

He bared his teeth. 'I drink the blood of young virgins,' he growled. 'It's much more effective.'

'Ugh, Guy! Stop pulling that face. You look like a pirate. You're making me feel quite nervous.'

And then Guy flung himself back down on the pillows and laughed richly. 'Your face...' he groaned at last. 'You really did look frightened...'

Jane felt sublimely happy. He was laughing, and for once she didn't feel that it put a painful distance between them. 'I was! I've never woken up in bed with a man before...I guess I was expecting you to look a bit, you know...dishevelled and needing a shave and so on. But nothing prepared me for the shock of going to bed with a clean-shaven man and waking up with a bearded one. I didn't know hair could grow that fast.'

'Should I have warned you? It never crossed my mind.'

'Yes! You had no right to give me a fright like that.'

'You looked very funny.'

'Well, it didn't feel the least bit funny, I can tell you. In fact, I don't think I'll ever be able to watch *A Midsummer Night's Dream* ever again. That bit where Bottom wakes up and he's got an ass's head . . . all rough and hairy . . . you know? His friends all get a dreadful fright and the audience always laugh its head off . . . Well, I shall close my eyes at that bit in future . . .'

' "Bless you, Bottom . . ." ' quoted Guy under his breath.

' "Thou art translated," ' she finished with a wry smile.

Guy frowned and then he propped himself up on one elbow and stared very intently at her. 'Good lord, Jane . . . this is very intellectual stuff . . . First you recognise a minor Pissarro and now you're quoting Shakespeare before I've even opened my eyes properly. Have you been deceiving me? Or hast thou been translated, too?' Strangely, he sounded as if he was accusing her.

Jane looked at him uncertainly. She always found it nearly impossible to read his face, and with that coating of dense, black stubble making him look so unfamiliar it was even more difficult. Was he impressed or dismayed? She pushed her hair back from her face with a flurried gesture. 'I haven't tried to deceive you about anything, Guy,' she said awkwardly. 'You're the one who's difficult to fathom. I'm not sure I shall ever understand you.'

'You don't try to understand me,' he said softly.

'I do!' she cried, remembering how hard she'd tried to see inside him. 'I honestly do. If I haven't asked the right questions, then I'm sorry.'

'You haven't asked any questions, Jane.'

She looked blankly at him. 'It hasn't been that sort of...relationship,' she muttered. 'We were always out, in company.'

'We sat at plenty of restaurant tables together. The other diners weren't in our laps. We talked about...nothing at all, really. Not me or you.'

'No, but...' she gulped. She had sensed the loneliness of his impoverished, loveless childhood only too clearly. And she had imagined Guy, later, when he had come to love her, lying in her arms, confiding it all because at last he needed to share it with her. That was how she yearned for it to be...how it *had* to be. 'Should I have asked you for a curriculum vitae? Is that what I should have done?' she demanded frantically. 'Would there have been any point, Guy? I've married the man you are now... What's past is past, isn't it? It's only the future we have to worry about.'

And then something horrible happened. Guy's eyes took on a severe, disapproving hue, and the planes of his face set themselves hard, and he got rapidly out of bed and strode to the bathroom, slamming the door behind him. She wanted to run after him and beg him to tell her what she had said to upset him. But, of course, she didn't. Their marriage wasn't like that, was it?

Instead she gathered her wrap about her and wandered along the landing until she found another bathroom, and showered briskly, washing her hair very vigorously. The next time they met up she was in the kitchen brewing coffee, her dressing-gown firmly belted, her wet hair brushed back from her face, and he was fully dressed and clean-shaven.

'What shall I get us to eat?' he asked. 'Do you want a full English breakfast? I arranged for some farm-cured bacon to be bought in, and there are plenty of eggs.'

'I think I'll just have some fruit,' she replied with a tight smile. 'This coffee's ready now. Shall I pour you a cup?'

Guy was squatting on his haunches in front of the fridge. 'Thanks,' he said absently, reaching in a hand to extract eggs and bacon. 'No sugar in mine.'

'I know,' she said painfully. 'I know you don't take sugar. We're married. I'm your wife now, remember?'

He straightened up and came across to her. In one hand he held a chilly package, wrapped in greaseproof paper, and in the other two cold eggs. He rested his forearms on her shoulders and crossed his wrists behind her neck. Then he stooped and kissed the top of her head. 'We've got an awful lot to learn, haven't we?' he said softly.

Jane let her cheek rest against the clean, crisp cotton of his short-sleeved shirt. 'I'm afraid we have,' she sighed wistfully. Then she looked up into his eyes and smiled. 'We have done the right thing, haven't we Guy?' she asked.

He smiled a slow smile then, and narrowed his eyes astutely. 'Of course we have,' he said crisply. 'My forte is getting things up and running, you know? I'll make a successful business of us in no time at all. Now run along and dry your hair while I cook this.'

Jane didn't know whether to be pleased or dismayed by his reassurance. The last thing she wanted was for their marriage to be run like a successful business, and yet she knew she should be glad that he was so obviously full of good intent. She made herself grin happily at him, and ducked out from under his arms. 'Give me the eggs and bacon,' she said cheerfully. 'I'll do the proper wifely bit and cook you breakfast.'

But Guy shook his head. 'I didn't marry you so that you could cook my breakfasts,' he said firmly. 'If I'd wanted a dumpy *hausfrau* I'd have chosen someone else.

I can do this myself. Now run along and put on a skimpy sundress and a bit of that gold eyeshadow which makes your eyes look so stunning, and get your hair dried. Breakfast will be ready in fifteen minutes in the courtyard.'

Jane wafted away disconsolately. She bit anxiously at the edge of one thumb as she stopped to survey the peasant-woman in the Pissarro picture, then she slowly mounted the stairs. How on earth did one set about making a marriage out of a business arrangement? Very gradually, she decided, as she dressed and dried her hair. Rome, after all, was not built in a day. And she could start right away by making herself look especially good.

After breakfast Guy continued to take charge.

'First,' he said, 'I shall show you around the gardens. And then you can take a good look at the house. You haven't seen it properly yet, have you? Then we can swim again, if you like. By then Fernanda and Palma will have finished cleaning and we can make love all afternoon.'

'Do we have to wait that long? Couldn't we telephone them and ask them not to come?'

He stretched lazily. 'We could but we won't. This is your honeymoon, remember?'

'Precisely.'

He paused, taking stock of her comment. 'Well, yes. It's your sexual initiation, and I understand how you must feel about that. But I don't want you to have to lift a finger, Jane, now that you're married to me. In fact, I rather hope you left all your clothes scattered on the bedroom floor for someone else to pick up.'

'I most certainly didn't!' She kept her voice light and teasing, but inside a wound was dripping blood. *Her* sexual initiation. Not *theirs*. Oh, he certainly wanted it to be good for *her* ... so that she would stay a good and loyal wife, no doubt. So that he could be seen to have done his duty. But for him it was nothing special ... and something of a bore, no doubt, to have such an inexperienced bride. One corner of her mouth puckered dangerously, but she managed to lift it into a smile. 'I'll...um...I'll chuck them all over the place tomorrow, if that's what you want. And I'll abandon coffee-cups in every room, too, and get talcum powder over everything and dump newspapers on the floor. Now come along and show me the gardens,' she said, tugging on his hand. 'We haven't got all day.'

The gardens were splendid, spreading over three or four acres, and screened from the surrounding vineyards by evergreens. Everywhere there were bright bursts of colour where flowers tumbled in profusion.

'It's fabulous!' she exclaimed as they sauntered down a shady, paved walk to a small pond with a fountain. 'All these trees—it's very well done, and properly mature, too. Just like a dream-garden should be.'

Guy nodded. 'It was designed by an Italian publishing giant, who had the house built to his own specification about forty years ago. I've had it for three or four years now... It's quite a gem, isn't it?'

'Mmmm. Though I have to say I don't like that fountain much. It seems silly and artificial, somehow. Everything else has been planted to look so natural... it jars a bit, though the sound of the water is nice. Perhaps there should be a little waterfall instead...? Though, of course, it would mean building a rockery for the water to cascade down...'

'The fountain,' said Guy evenly, 'is perfectly natural, as it happens. It's a spring, which shoots up out of the rock below. It goes much higher in March and April, and dies away to little more than a trickle in September, before the autumn rains begin.'

'Oh,' said Jane feeling unaccountably stupid. 'I didn't realise that.'

'We could get the rock blasted away and divert the spring to come out on top of an artificial rockery, if you like. This is your garden. You can make any changes you want.'

Jane put her hand instinctively to her throat, where his words seemed to lie, razor-sharp, against her fine skin. Guy, quite obviously, didn't want her to change anything. 'No. Don't be silly. Of course not . . . I love it now that I know that it's . . . it's a spring.' She tailed away and cleared her throat.

She couldn't help thinking of her mother struggling against the heavy clay soil in her own garden, happy and fulfilled despite the paucity of her results. That was the sort of wife that she had always vaguely assumed that she would be, when her time came—working hard to make everything grow—to get it right. But this garden was perfect already.

Later, she discovered that the house, when she had peered into every nook and cranny and explored every room, was equally perfect. There were seven bedrooms, and not one of them furnished with bits and pieces which no one could bear to throw away, but which didn't quite fit. They all looked as if they had been freshly dressed to have their pictures taken for a glossy magazine. Downstairs was even more tasteful. The biggest reception room was at least thirty feet long, and so light and airy and sunny that cool white blinds had been half-drawn over the windows to diffuse the brilliant light. They did their job perfectly, and even managed to look chic in the process. Jane remembered the light bulbs and turned away.

She sauntered over to the fireplace and surveyed the painting which hung there. It was a restful landscape of snow-capped mountains, backlit by a wintry sky. 'That's beautiful,' she said. 'Is it a local scene?'

Guy stuck his hands in the pockets of his trousers and surveyed it from the other side of the room. 'No,' he said. 'It isn't.'

But he didn't offer any more information and she didn't ask. She sensed an air of annoyance gathering about him again and was anxious to change the mood.

'Have Fernanda and Palma gone yet?' she asked.

'Why? Are you hungry? They've set out our lunch outdoors...'

'I'm not hungry for food,' she replied mischievously. 'Can we go and explore our bedroom again? I think it's my favourite room, you know...?'

And it worked, because Guy stopped giving off vibes of annoyance, and strode swiftly across the room towards her. He pulled her to him, and without bothering to reply kissed her every bit as fiercely and demandingly as he had in the car park, when he'd kissed her for the very first time. He had courted her and wed her and wooed her. At last, it seemed, he was prepared to simply enjoy here. Jane quivered with excitement. Rome might not have been built in a day—but it was only lunchtime and already she'd made progress...

When they were clinging to each other on the bed, discarding clothes in the process, Jane whispered, 'Show me what to do...to please you, Guy...'

He paid no attention to her request, but simply started to kiss her so hard that she forgot to feel hurt.

Later, when they were lying on top of the covers, both naked and bathed in sweat, after a brief, urgent, and highly satisfactory coupling, Jane had to blink away tears of happiness. None of yesterday's lessons had been needed as she had been carried forward on a wave of such ruthless desire that the whole world had seemed to crack apart as he moved within her. Instinct had provided all the tutoring she needed, and his satiated frame, spreadeagled beside her, left her in no doubt that she was, after all, in one respect at least, proving to be a very satisfactory wife.

Tentatively she reached out one hand and ran her fingers through his hair. It was damp near the roots.

'I enjoyed that,' she said happily.

'Mmmm...' he grunted, not moving.

Jane let her eyes drift to the open window overlooking the front garden. In the distance she could see the cedars standing still in the hazy summer air. Where they parted, at the entrance to the drive, she saw two figures pushing bicycles out of the gate and into the road.

'There are Fernanda and Palma...' she exclaimed, surprised. 'They're only just leaving.'

Guy reluctantly dragged a wrist in front of his eyes. 'Twelve o'clock,' he sighed. 'Yes, that's right.'

Jane hugged her arms around her naked breasts, shivering with pleasure. So he hadn't been able to wait for the help to leave? He *wanted* her. He really did. Oh, she would do everything in her power to make him happy. Everything.

For the rest of the day they swam—naked at one point—and ate, and drank wine and kissed.

'I'm so happy,' she told Guy seriously, as they lay together in bed. 'You were right. We are good together, aren't we?'

And he looked at her and smiled in return and said, 'I told you we would be.' And then he rubbed his freshly shaven chin against her forehead, and held her close to him while they fell asleep.

The next day was idyllic. They drove through the Tuscan hills on empty roads and visited Siena and returned to an empty house which they filled with the sounds of their lovemaking. Later, in the garden, Jane looked up through the leaves of a fig tree at the pale blue sky and almost shouted with joy. This place was heaven on earth. When she went indoors to change she studied the painting of the peasant-woman and thought of Guy's roots, and her own, and she felt that, together, they might grow something very good in this fertile soil. It was going to work.

Three more lazy days in the sun followed. But the day after that the sky was splotched with clouds too white in the centre, and a raggedy grey at the edges.

'I don't think the weather's going to hold up,' commented Guy over breakfast. 'I'll tell you what...I'll take you into Florence. We've got all day.'

Jane shook her head so that her dark hair swung around her face. 'No, we haven't. We've only got the morning. I agree it would be awful sitting in the house doing nothing while the place is cleaned. But I've no complaint about being closeted here with you all afternoon, alone, while it pours down outside.'

Guy smiled. 'Let's pray for rain when we get back, then. But we might as well take our time in Florence once we get there. I've got a few things planned which I think will give you pleasure of a different sort. Now go and get ready.'

She dressed carefully, pinning up her hair so that the cleverly cut ends sprayed out into a fan on the top of her head. It was a youthful, exuberant style and one of which she was particularly fond. It looked especially good with the grey and white striped seersucker trousers she wore, teamed with a cropped matching silk blouse which showed her slender brown midriff to perfection.

'You look great,' said Guy appreciatively, slipping on a blue linen jacket and checking his pockets. 'Now hurry up. I've got a lot planned for today.'

Jane sank into the passenger seat of the car and settled back for the ride. 'What shall we look at first?' she said happily. 'There's so much to see.'

'How many times have you been to Florence?'

'Twice. I love it. I went once with my parents ages and ages ago, and then last year I came out with some friends.'

'Tell me about these friends,' invited Guy, his eyes on the road ahead.

Jane bit her lip. She had come with the Berringtons, as it happened. She wondered, not for the first time, why such dreadful snobs should have wanted her for a friend—and why they had kept their opinions to themselves for so long. Since that fateful evening she hadn't seen them, and had pointedly not invited them to the wedding. She had certainly never mentioned them in front of Guy. The best thing, she decided, was to talk about them as if the argument had been nothing but a silly tiff. Although he claimed to have heard a little of what was said, he certainly hadn't heard the terrible things Benedicta had said about him inside the car, and she didn't want him prying into it all now.

'Well, they're twins. Benedicta and Charlotte. Er...I think you met them once...? Anyway, they're identical and...um...very lively. We came with one of their sisters, Rosalind—they've got five older sisters, actually. And their brother Rupert came too. He's only ten months younger than they are. So they're all very close.'

'Uh-huh...' said Guy. 'Wasn't Rupert rather overpowered with four older women to keep him in line?'

Jane shook her head. 'Actually, he wasn't the only male. Rosalind and the twins all brought boyfriends along. Rosalind's engaged to hers now. He's really nice, but a bit shy, and the twins used to tease him by pretending to be each other all the time.'

She noticed Guy's eyebrows curve upwards dangerously, and his mouth had returned to the straight, formal line she had seen so often until he had decided to marry her. He clearly wasn't impressed by her account so far.

'It was pretty stupid, I guess,' she admitted, feeling suddenly very silly and juvenile. 'But Charles—that's Rosalind's fiancé—well, he took it all in good part. He didn't mind. Not really.'

'And what about Rupert?'

'What about him?'

'Was he just along for the ride, or what?'

She looked at his profile uncertainly. 'Er…not exactly. He and I…we were…well, we kept each other company. We were…um…sort of going out with each other at the time. We did for quite a long while, actually, except that as he lived in Sussex and I lived in the Midlands we didn't see very much of each other for weeks on end. It was never serious, actually. Not a bit. Ever.'

Jane had enjoyed the platonic relationship. Not just because Rupert was good company, but because it had kept other men from smarming all over her. Being beautiful wasn't always easy.

Was Guy jealous? She glanced sideways at him, finding herself stupidly hoping that he would be.

But in fact he looked quite unperturbed. 'He must be younger than you, then?'

She sighed. It would have been nice if Guy had been just a tiny bit jealous, even though he had no cause. 'About two months younger. Yes.'

'Is he the youngest?'

'Yes. His poor mother finally produced a boy. Seven girls and then, at last, the son they needed for the title. Once he was born she handed him over to a nanny and went on holiday all by herself for a month. She said she'd earned it.'

'What would have happened to the title if she'd never had a boy?'

'I don't know. I've never asked about that. I suppose it would have gone to some cousin or something. Or maybe the oldest daughter's first son? Can titles skip generations like that?'

Guy shrugged. 'Why should I know something like that?'

'Dear me, Guy,' she tutted. 'You can't have been keeping your eyes and ears open ... I thought you knew *everything*.'

Guy chuckled. 'It's not a question of eyes and ears. I only pick up information that's likely to be of use to me. Anything that I hand on to my children will be handed on of my own free will. If I want there to be strings attached, then they will be strings of my own devising. I make up my own traditions as I go along, Jane. Or hadn't you realised that?'

'Oh, yes. Of course,' said Jane, and then swallowed. 'Um ... how many sons or daughters were you planning on?' She felt flustered all of a sudden.

'How many were you?' he asked drily.

'Um ... well, not eight.'

'No,' he agreed, clearly amused. 'Not eight. Nine or seven, maybe ... but not eight.'

'No! Nine or seven? Not really?'

'No. Not really.'

'Oh. Good. I don't think I could manage that many. Though Lady Alicia did, and she always looked marvellous.'

'She had nannies, though, you said?'

'Oh yes. Three at any one time. She could afford it, though ...' And then her voice faded as she realised that Guy, too, could afford it.

'Three nannies ...' murmured Guy, drolly. 'And how many babies could you manage with four nannies, Jane? Or five?'

'You're teasing me, aren't you?' asked Jane primly.

'But of course. One nanny will be quite sufficient, I should think. Shouldn't you?'

'Do we have to have a nanny at all?'

'Certainly we do,' said Guy, and his voice was suddenly harsh.

And Jane said, 'Well, in that case . . . yes. One nanny sounds just fine.'

But she said it through clenched teeth because her mother hadn't had so much as one nanny. Her mother had sent her father out of the hotel to find somewhere to buy feeding bottles and formula and nappies and hundreds of other things, and had nursed her baby in her arms all by herself—and she wouldn't put her down even when the police came, nor the doctor—and she had carried her all the way to the hospital, snuggled close against her own, dry breast. Her mother had never wanted a nanny. Jane had never imagined having a nanny for her children, either.

Their first stop in Florence was a Lancia car showroom, where Jane's car was ordered.

'What colour?' asked the salesman, handing Jane a colour chart.

But Guy flicked it out of her hands. 'We can have it customised,' he said. 'Choose any colour you like. You look good with strong colours, Jane . . . that bikini you had on the other day suited you—and your anorak.'

'Guy!' she exclaimed, half horrified, half-pleased. 'I've heard of people changing their car when the ashtrays get full, but ordering one to match their bikini has to be about the height of decadence.'

'It has to be some colour or other. Why not have a colour you like—or a colour which likes you? That's all I'm suggesting. And as for it being decadent, well, it keeps people employed. What's decadent about that?'

'Well . . .'

'Well, which colour? We'll never make it back to the villa this afternoon if you keep dithering.'

'Put like that . . . well, how does lilac sound?'

'Disgusting. But if it's what you want...'

'It is.'

'Great. And what about the upholstery?' he asked.

Jane shrugged. 'Is there a choice? When I got my Metro it just sort of arrived and the upholstery was the colour it was.'

'Cream leather? White plastic? Diamanté-studded leopardskin?'

'Oh. With lilac?'

'It'll have to be cream leather, won't it? Serves you right for choosing such a revolting colour.'

'I suppose it will,' she laughed.

And so the car was purchased, and then shoes, and handbags to match the shoes and then clothes to match the handbags. They ended up at the Ponte Vecchio, elegantly straddling the river Arno, and clustered on either side with jewellers' shops—all of which Guy seemed determined to clear of stock. She only had to stop to study some item and he nodded at the assistant and the item was hers. Every time they strolled out of a shop and into the fresh, blustery air Jane would look longingly towards the Uffizi, situated just beyond the bridge. There were paintings in there which made every single item they bought today seem like so much dross. But Guy didn't even seem to see the gallery, let alone suggest a visit.

In the end she said longingly, 'Oughtn't we go into the Uffizi, now that we're so near?'

Guy slung his arm around her shoulder and pulled her close to him. 'You're very well brought up, aren't you?'

'What do you mean?'

'I mean, I bet when you came before, you armed yourself with guide books and ticked off items as you saw them, didn't you?'

'No. I really love paintings, Guy.'

'I'll bet.'

'Does that mean you don't want to go in?'

'I want to get you home and see if I can create a little more employment.'

'Employment?'

'Mmmm. You know...a job-creation scheme for an unemployed nanny.'

'Oh.' Jane burned with embarrassment. 'You mean you want to make a baby?'

'Got it in one.'

'Are you serious?'

'Deadly.'

'I...um...Guy, I went on the Pill while you were in Malaysia.'

He was silent for a moment, and then relaxed his hold on her. 'Now why on earth didn't you think to mention that before?'

'I...I thought you would have just assumed... You know, I didn't make a secret of it on purpose. They're in the bathroom cabinet.'

'Ah, well...obviously I wasn't keeping my eyes as wide open as I ought to have done. Never mind. We can still practise for when the time comes, can't we?'

'Oh. Yes. Yes...there's nothing I'd like better.' She was silent for a moment and then managed to stutter, 'Didn't you think I would be on the Pill? It seemed like the right thing to do. I didn't know you wanted a baby right away.'

Guy straightened up and let his arm drop to his side. 'It's OK, Jane. It's your decision, after all. I guess I should have talked about these things sooner and found out where you stood.'

There was a silence and then Jane bit out, 'Like when we were sitting across the table from each other in all those restaurants? It takes two to talk about nothing at all, you know.'

Guy flinched. 'Touché,' he said coldly.

'Is that why you married me?' she asked uncertainly, her blood chilling in her veins. 'To have a...son and heir?'

'Goddammit, Jane, what's the matter with you? You're talking as if marriage and babies had nothing whatsoever to do with each other.'

'They don't,' she snapped. 'Not these days. Not in England in the 1990s. Plenty of career women get married with no idea in their minds of having babies. And plenty of single women go ahead and have babies with no idea of ever getting married.'

'But you stressed the first time we met that you were no career woman?'

'Oh.' Jane's blood positively froze. 'So you immediately assumed that the only alternative I had in mind was making babies as hard and fast as I could? No wonder I must have seemed like the perfect wife for you, Guy. In this day and age I must be something of a rarity.'

'So what was the alternative form of marriage you had in mind? Dabbling in art appreciation classes? Swanning off to Stratford to catch up on the RSC's latest production? Taking in a little culture on the side to keep the dinner party conversations flowing—to help steer the men away from boring old shop talk?'

'I...I don't believe this! I don't! Look, I genuinely love art. And Shakespeare. I certainly don't cultivate them as useful social attributes. And I didn't marry you so that I could have someone to take me to the opera.'

'What a shame. I have tickets for La Scala, next week. *Rigoletto*. Don't you want to go?'

'Not if you're going to use it as a stick to beat me with.'

'Now why should I do that, Jane? You're my wife now. The social life is part of the grand scheme, isn't it? We'll go to Milan and stay somewhere nice and dine in the most expensive place and we'll enjoy ourselves immensely at the opera,' he said bitterly.

Jane sighed. 'I'm sorry,' she muttered. 'I'm sorry that there have been these misunderstandings between us when you wanted everything to be crystal clear from the start. It hardly seems fair. Of course I'll go to the opera with you. I'll enjoy it very much.' The last time she had seen *Rigoletto* she had cried her eyes out. It was unbearably sad. 'It all sounds perfect. Thank you very much for thinking of it.'

'The pleasure,' said Guy sarcastically, 'will be all mine.'

CHAPTER EIGHT

THE trouble was, Jane reflected as they drove back in silence, that she was, after all, a modern Englishwoman. Mumtaz had assimilated the rules from birth—she knew exactly how arranged marriages should be. Whereas Jane had taken all her preconceptions about love and romance with her into this arrangement with Guy. Now that she thought about it, producing an heir was bound to be part of the deal. Jane yearned quite desperately to have Guy's child. Once he loved her, of course. She was quite sure of that. She was less certain of her ability to produce an heir to order. It just didn't feel right.

Patience, she reminded herself wearily...that was all it needed. She looked across at him. It was still early days...but it *would* happen; she was sure of it. Her heart ached to think of him growing up with so little love. Guy had never had anyone who put his needs first. When he realised that she was ready to put him first always—when he saw how willing she was to please him, then those ties which bound his emotions so tight would surely loosen. One day they would lie in each other's arms and spill out all their dreams and laugh—together.

Back at the villa she watched Guy diving, somersaulting in what looked like a horribly dangerous fashion before slicing into the deep water. She waited for him to surface, frightened in case he had hit his head on the bottom. When he burst through the rippling blue water in a froth of white bubbles her heart jumped with relief.

'Come on...' he said, getting out of the water and making his way back to the boards. 'Let me teach you...'

But Jane shook her head. 'I've already told you... I don't want to learn to do fancy diving.'

'Are you afraid?' he asked considerately, stopping and turning towards her.

But she simply shook her head again.

'Then why not? You dive nicely off the side. You could be good.'

She shrugged. 'I... it's not my kind of thing.'

He sighed. 'Then what is your kind of thing?'

'I just want to be happy. To enjoy life, Guy. I've told you that before.'

'And diving would put a stop to that?'

'No. Of course not. It's just... oh, dear, I can't explain it. I just don't see the point in striving to do things like that for their own sake... I never have done. I'm not like you, you see. Everything you do, you do to perfection, don't you?'

'Oddly enough, that isn't really true. I try to do things well only because it gives me pleasure. If the results are good then it owes more to luck than deliberation.'

She looked steadily at him. 'You may not deliberately set out to achieve great things, Guy. Or at least, you may not think that you do. But it's no accident that you *always* get exactly what you want from life. You set exceptionally high standards for yourself. They're there, working away beneath the surface, all the time. And they bring success in their wake whether you want to acknowledge it or not. You'll always be successful, Guy. You'll always get exactly what you want.'

Guy looked at her quizzically. Then he said, 'Does that mean you'll come off the Pill?'

'Not yet. I... I don't feel quite ready yet. But I *will* have our baby. When the time comes.'

'Don't you want children, Jane?'

Jane nodded slowly. 'I do. I really do. Eventually.'

'Then why do you want to wait?' asked Guy slowly.

'Because . . . because I just don't feel . . .' She sighed. 'Just give me time to come to terms with it all. OK?'

And Guy put a wet arm around her shoulder and held her close to him and said no more.

That evening Guy cooked her yet another meal.

'Let me cook it,' she pleaded.

'Why? Don't you like my cooking?'

'Yes. Of course I do. But I can cook, too.'

But he just shrugged and went on dicing green peppers with a very sharp knife.

The next day he seemed irritable and impatient, and suggested driving down to the coast. They ended up on a beautiful, half-empty beach. No sooner had they settled themselves on the sand that Guy went off and hired a sailboard. 'Do you want to do some windsurfing, too?' he asked.

Jane shook her head. 'No. I don't know how. I've never tried.'

'I'll show you,' he volunteered.

She hesitated for a moment. This was an opportunity to show him that she was willing to strive at something—to attempt, at least, to match his exacting standards—and to please him . . . She produced a smile from somewhere and said, 'Great. I'll enjoy that.'

In order to teach her he had to touch her. They stood waist-deep in water while he showed her where to put her hands and feet, and helped her squirm on to the board in order to get the feel of it. She wanted to shout out her love and grab hold of his big, wet shoulders and kiss him, and be held by him, there in the sea with the sailboards keeling towards them, their brilliantly coloured sails flapping about their heads.

Instead she concentrated on his instructions, and stood back admiringly while he demonstrated with his own board.

In fact, she learned well and was managing to stay upright for quite creditable periods of time by the end of the day. Disappointment, rejection, frustration—these, it seemed, were the keys to achievement. If Guy had travelled that route, then it wouldn't hurt her to follow. It would bring them closer. Surely she would please him far more that way than by simply wallowing in the animal contentment that came from being his wife?

On the way back he asked, 'Did you enjoy the windsurfing, Jane?'

'Yes,' she responded, surprised to find that it was the truth. 'It was exhilarating—when I wasn't falling off, that is.'

'It's a good sport, isn't it?'

'Yes.'

'So you're glad you made the effort?'

'Yes, Guy. You were right, after all.'

You always are, she found herself thinking. But does that mean that I'm always wrong? Does it mean that you won't learn to love me? And then she remembered Mumtaz wagging a finger at her and saying, 'True love can only grow from respect, Jane...' and she girded her loins.

'Er...do you...um...do you respect me for trying?' she asked.

Guy turned his head briefly from the road, and stole a glance at her. 'What a funny question...'

'Do you, though?'

'Yes. If you put it like that, I suppose I do.'

The next day they returned to the same beach for water-skiing lessons. Jane coped well with this, too. However, she found it quite exhausting, and was relieved to return to her sun-lounger and toast her brown skin a deeper shade of brown while she watched Guy slice across the blue crescent of the bay in the wake of the speed-boat. At last he returned and flopped on to the sand beside her, making his sleek, shining body gritty with sand.

'You've been pebble-dashed,' she said.

He tried to brush the sand away but it stuck to his wet hand. He smiled. 'I've heard of people being built like houses, but never of someone being rendered like one.'

Jane trailed her fingers in the sand and then suddenly picked up a handful and scattered it playfully over his broad back. 'Some are born rendered,' she intoned dramatically. 'Some achieve rendering, and others have render thrust upon them...' And then she slapped his big shoulders and rubbed the sand hard against his skin.

Guy flashed her a rare, broad smile. He was clearly amused. But she was disappointed. She had rather hoped to make him laugh for once.

'You certainly know your Shakespeare,' he said.

'I love Shakespeare,' she smiled. 'I go to Stratford whenever I can—but I like reading him, too. We had to read the plays at school. Except for the rude bits, of course—we weren't expected to know the rude bits. We were given expurgated versions at school.'

He had buried his face in a towel and was rubbing at his hair. 'You mean your school censored Shakespeare? Good grief. And they call that an education?' he muttered wryly.

'It doesn't seem to have done me much harm,' Jane laughed. 'After all, I seem to be managing the unexpurgated version of married life very well—despite my lack of formal education.'

'Only because you've got such a good personal tutor...' Guy returned, his eyes sharp with amusement, and then he threw down the towel and knelt beside her and kissed her.

It was the first time he had kissed her in a public place—except for the wedding service, which didn't count because he had no choice—and she felt weak at the knees with delight. Because it must mean something. Mustn't it?

When he stopped kissing her he flopped back on the sand and closed his eyes. Jane felt happier than she could ever remember feeling.

'What shall we do now?' he asked at last.

Jane opened her eyes very wide and said, 'Don't you ever get tired?'

Guy shook his head. 'Not when I'm doing water sports,' he replied. 'Especially water-skiing. I love speed, Jane.'

She wrinkled up her nose disapprovingly. 'Now don't you do anything dangerous.'

Guy let out a relaxed, sardonic laugh. 'And don't you start turning into a nagging wife.'

'Huh. Do you think it's likely, Guy? What would be the point? I can't see you being susceptible to nagging.'

'Perhaps not... But if you didn't mean to nag, then why did you say it?'

'I was just——' Just frightened of losing you. Because I love you. She stopped herself with difficulty. The sun and the sand, the laughter and the relaxation, and the kiss... They could so easily have seduced her into giving far too much away... 'Well, I just don't want to have to cope with an accident, that's all. I don't speak Italian, for a start.'

Guy sighed. 'Don't worry. I don't have any desire to put my life on the line. In fact, that's why I like water-skiing so much. It feels fast and dangerous, but it's very safe as long as you follow the rules.'

'I certainly feel safe enough when you drive,' remarked Jane. 'At least you don't indulge your love of speed behind the wheel of the car.'

'Ha! That's where you're wrong. You've only been for a ride in one of my new cars, Jane. But I've got several 1960s sports cars, too. You know, the small ones which were so popular then? None of them is in mint-condition—to put it mildly—though of course I make sure that they're well maintained. But I also make sure they still suffer from the odd bump and rattle. Then, with the hood down, on a sunny day, they provide the perfect ride. I only need to get up to about forty miles an hour to feel as if I'm about to take off into space. And by the time I hit the speed limit I feel as if I'm at Silverstone!'

He paused for a moment and then added, 'I satisfy my needs these days by substituting the illusion for the real thing. And it works just beautifully. Clever, huh?'

And then Jane opened her enormous, dark eyes and looked at him and found herself quite unable to reply. Because all of a sudden she understood that she was like one of those old cars to him. A safe substitute for the real thing. She was being tinkered with in the interests of creating the perfect illusion. Wind-surfing and water-skiing, customised cars and seats at La Scala...but he didn't want her to cook or make a home for him or do any of the things a real wife should do. True, she would be allowed to bear him his child—as long as she handed it over to a substitute mother as soon as it was born. Presumably, then, the illusion would be complete. In his eyes it would have all worked out just beautifully. Clever, huh?

The trip to Milan was wonderful. The opera was everything she had remembered, and suberbly produced. She recited her times-tables in her head towards the end and concentrated on the orchestra and managed not to cry. Later, she would remember not to talk about it either.

When the applause had finally died away she turned to Guy and smiled and said, 'That was marvellous. I did enjoy it.'

And when the house lights went up and she looked around, she was pleased to discover that none of the other glittering young wives was crying, either. Now wasn't she doing well?

The rest of the week they stayed at the villa, loafing around and making love. Then, one afternoon, after they had eaten lunch and drunk wine at the poolside, and Guy had demolished *The Times* and the *Financial Times*—which had mysteriously started appearing—he scratched the hairs on his chest and then stretched, and said, 'I've got a few phone calls to make, Jane. Will you be OK for the rest of the afternoon?'

Jane nodded. 'Go ahead. I think I'm about to fall asleep, anyway.'

But in fact the moment he had gone indoors she felt horribly wide awake and alone and insecure. She wandered around the garden. She admired the plants she hadn't planted, and the grass she hadn't mown and watered and fed. In the end she wandered into the house, ostensibly to find a book, but in reality just to be physically close to Guy.

She could hear his voice, muffled, through the door of his study, gravelly and deep. She took a shower and came back downstairs. Still his voice could be heard, animated, authoritative, while she stood silent and barefoot, like an eavesdropper in the tiled hallway. She padded off and made a coffee very slowly before returning to the hall. Still Guy's voice murmured through the empty space. She mustn't mind that he had work to do. He'd given her a fortnight of his precious time, after all. Jane went back out to the garden.

When she drifted back in, chilled by the lengthening shadows of the cypress trees, Guy had put potatoes in the fan-assisted oven to bake, and was making a salad.

'How did it go this afternoon?' she asked.

Guy leant back against the sink, his hands gripping the shining chrome edge behind him. 'OK. I've tied up a few loose ends in Kuala Lumpur.'

'Oh. How clever,' she found herself saying sharply. 'I didn't realise they had telephones in Kuala Lumpur.'

He frowned at her and pulled a face.

'Um...sorry. I wasn't concentrating...' she added apologetically, biting her tongue. This was no way to earn his respect. 'Of course they've got telephones in Kuala Lumpur...'

He looked away, then continued evenly. 'I can't finalise everything over the phone, though. I'll have to go back out there before long and check things over.'

Jane reached up and twisted one of her earrings rather more vigorously than usual. 'Uh-huh. Fine. Terrific.'

'And I've arranged a house party.'

'A house party? Here?'

'Mmmm. Next week. I've invited five couples to stay in the house with us. They're all top-brass from Rexford Holdings, so you'll need to get to know them sooner or later. I thought it would be a good opportunity.'

'Great...'

'They'll drift up to the house in dribs and drabs on Saturday—we can sort out a buffet of some sort to cope with that. And then I thought we'd do a barbecue on the Saturday night—I'll see to that, so no problem... though perhaps you could organise a few puddings? And then a sort of communal breakfast before they drift away again on the Sunday? What do you think?'

Jane, actually, thought it sounded bloody awful. For a start, she didn't know any of these people...though,

ironically, she was to be allowed to cook for *them*. More
importantly, she wanted to keep Guy all to herself on
her honeymoon . . . so did this mean the honeymoon was
over? It must do . . . real married life was about to begin.

What she said was, 'Fantastic, Guy! Absolutely
brilliant . . . it sounds like a wonderful idea,' with such
enthusiasm that she almost made herself laugh. Well,
almost . . .

He wanted a wife who could handle the social side
with panache? Jolly good. Then with panache she would
handle it. He would never fall in love with her if she
didn't keep to her side of the bargain.

The next day she followed Guy down to the diving
pool with pen and paper in her hand and dangled her
feet in the water, shouting questions at Guy who was
flexing his muscles on the very high top board.

'What size are the women?'

'Jane?'

'I said what size are the women?'

He executed a perfect double somersault which made
her stomach churn. When he broke the surface she
explained, 'I want to make sure that there's a selection
of swimsuits in case anyone forgets, or needs to borrow
one for some reason. So what size are the women?'

Guy laughed, sluicing the water off his face with his
hands. 'One extremely large. Two sort of a bit mumsy
around the chest these days. And two skinny.'

'Hayfever?'

'Pardon?'

'Flowers for their rooms. Does anyone suffer from
hayfever that you know of?'

'Maxine's always snivelling,' he said amiably as he
remounted the steps. 'But I think that's got more to do
with the fact that Liam's incorrigibly unfaithful than
the state of her sinuses.'

'Good. And are there any alcoholics among them, or can I be as heavy-handed with the punch as I'd like to be?'

`Hmm. She was doing well. She hadn't known she could be so good at this sort of thing. Guy had been right, once again.

'No. No alcoholics. Helen's a teetotaller, though.'

'I'll do a fruit-cup as well, then.'

Plop. A jack-knife of such exceptional tautness that she wanted to jump in the pool with him, tear those black trunks off him and kiss all the wetness from his face and say, 'Let's cancel the party and make love all weekend instead.' As it happened she had no need. Guy surfaced, grabbed hold of her wrist and pulled her in, peeling off her T-shirt and tugging at her shorts while she flailed in the water, shrieking and laughing. She was becoming the sort of wife he wanted and he loved it! Hip hip hooray! A few more foundation stones were in place. Now all she had to do was to resist the temptation to throw them at his head.

She spent every morning of the following week making lists and shopping and stuffing olives by hand. She arranged for Palma and Fernanda to come in all day on the Friday. She bought herself a simple little gold evening dress with next-to-no back, which, before her marriage, would have left her with next-to-no bank balance, and a super, baggy, grass-green pyjama suit for the breakfast party. She saw to everything. Exotic fruits tumbled from exotic bowls, naptha flares sprang up among the flowers like a blight, and stacks of monogrammed white towels lurked in cupboards like spies, waiting to replace the monogrammed white towels on duty, just as soon as the first boring guest had powdered her shiny, intrusive nose.

The weekend went off perfectly. Guy was as perfect a host as Jane was a hostess. Everybody laughed a lot and swam a lot and ate a lot and danced a lot. Nobody drank too much and Maxine didn't snivel. One of the substitute bathing costumes was indeed needed, highlighting most effectively Jane's superlative qualities as a hostess, and fresh towels kept appearing as if by magic. Jane did not once stop the men from talking shop. And everybody, but everybody, said time and again how beautiful Jane was and how clever Jane was and didn't Jane make just the perfect wife for Guy. *Didn't she just...?*

When they had gone Guy kissed her very deeply and murmured, 'You were wonderful.'

'So were you.'

'You're still wonderful.'

She squirmed against him, laying her face against his chest. 'So are you.'

'Shall we go upstairs and see if we can be even more wonderful for each other?'

'Mmmm...'

Afterwards, he said, 'You thrive in company, don't you? Isn't it too quiet for you here?'

Her heart lurched. 'No,' she said insistently. 'I love it.'

'It's a magical place, isn't it?'

'Yes.' So he had noticed it too? Good...

'I'm going to have to start commuting. I can't leave Rexford Holdings to its own devices for much longer.'

Not so good. 'Of course not.'

'You'll be lonely.'

Jane shook her head vigorously. *Please* don't let him suggest that they leave! She wanted to spend as much time here with Guy as was possible. Everything was going so well. All they needed was time...more time...she would be the wife he thought he wanted, until one day he would realise that he loved her—and then she would be the wife he really wanted, and there would be no more

illusions. Ever. 'There's an English club near Siena. I'll
soon make friends.'

'Won't you be bored?'

'Oh, not for a while. Not in summer. I'm dying to go
back to Florence, for a start. And there's that golf-course
we pass on the way to the beach...I'd thought of learning
golf. Anyway, now the season's getting under way the
beaches will be packed. I thought I'd enrol for water-
skiing lessons—so I'm bound to get to know lots of
people, aren't I?'

He sighed. 'If you're sure...'

'I am.'

Life began to mould itself into shape. Guy spent three
days a week at the villa—and four in London. Well,
usually. Sometimes he was in Malaysia or Stuttgart or
Glasgow. It didn't make much difference to Jane. When
he was away he didn't call. But she was learning well.
She didn't make any more snide comments about the
telephones—or lack of them—in such places.

While he was away she tried rearranging the furniture,
but discovered, to her disappointment, that it had been
just perfect the way it was. The summer drifted by. This
was marriage—real and earnest. Guy was good at it. Jane
was good at it. Two whole months of it slid away. One
day Guy said, 'Have you thought any more about having
a baby?'

Jane twisted the diamond stud in her ear and smiled.
'Mmmm. I like the idea, Guy. I really do. But...
er...well...I don't want to go ahead yet for a while.'

'It's your choice, Jane. Whenever you're ready. I'm
sorry if I seem impatient.'

'When I'm ready I'll let you know.'

'You're not frightened of childbirth or anything, are
you?'

'No.'

'Or of losing your figure?'

'No! Of course not.'

'Or of pregnancy itself? Some women don't like the idea of——'

'I'm not frightened of pregnancy, Guy.'

'Oh. Then what is it, Jane? Can't you explain?'

She felt guilty. He wanted her to provide him with a child so badly, and she loved him and wanted so much to give him his heart's desire. She looked into his eyes. 'It's difficult to explain, Guy,' she sighed, and suddenly, to her horror, her eyes filled up with tears. She blinked fast. 'It's just very difficult. It's something that goes deep. But I promise you, Guy... I promise you that just as soon as I feel ready then we'll go ahead.'

Guy looked at her so longingly then that her heart leapt and she almost shouted, 'Now! I'm ready now!'

But then his eyes turned grey and he stroked her hand and said with his usual control, 'Take your time. There's no rush.'

But there was. Because if he didn't start to love her soon she had a horrible feeling she wouldn't be able to go on with this marriage. She had convinced herself that because she loved him it was all somehow meant to be. But she wasn't sure that she could handle it, after all. At any rate, she couldn't bring herself to have this baby, which was clearly in the rules, and which she couldn't put off for ever.

If only she had another culture to refer to, to give her strength. Once, long ago, there had been a whole class of Englishwomen who had known the rules, in the days of empire, and country-house parties and—the mistresses hidden discreetly from view. But that was another culture too. Those women had passed away. There was no one to tell Jane what she could expect. And the isolation was profound.

CHAPTER NINE

AND then one day Guy came back to the villa from New York, with a New Yorker in the car. A female New Yorker, tall and blonde and ravishing.

'Hi there!' She strode towards Jane on long, lean legs, smiling a smile of toothpastey perfection, and not waiting to be introduced. 'You must be Jane. Guy's told me all about you. I'm just thrilled to meet you, Jane.'

'This is Ella Franklin, Jane,' said Guy with an urbane smile. 'She's a lawyer. We hadn't completed our work, so I invited her out here for a few days so we could finish off.'

'I'm very pleased to meet you, Ella,' said Jane, creating a neat little smile of her own, while praying that jealousy wasn't shooting out of her eyeballs like green lasers. 'You must be very tired. Do come on in and you can freshen up.'

'Oh, but I'm feeling just great,' said Ella, beaming. 'Guy's kept me wide awake all the way over. This man is just *so* amusing. We've been laughing all the way from Kennedy through to your front door—haven't we, Guy?'

Guy smiled and said nothing, but he came and put his arm around Jane in a very husbandly fashion. It didn't help.

Jane widened her smile. By now the three of them could have been advertising competing brands of toothpaste, judging by the number of teeth on view. She nipped on her lower lip to make sure her own particular version didn't turn into a pathetic smirk. 'Then you must let me get you a cool drink,' she murmured hospitably. 'It's so hot out here at this time of the year.'

Inside the house Ella stopped in front of the Pissarro and let out a low whistle. 'That's some painting.'

'It's a Pissarro,' said Jane.

'Wow... I've even heard of him! Hey, but I thought he only did landscape?'

Drat. Ella Franklin wasn't just a hot-shot lawyer; she wasn't even just an intelligent lady mature enough to share a joke with Guy; the wretched creature was *cultured* as well!

'He was very prolific,' Jane explained, suddenly frantic to display her superior knowledge. 'He certainly concentrated on landscapes for many years, but what is less well-known is that he turned to peasant subjects later when he——'

'Let's get that drink. I'm parched,' interrupted Guy, gripping Jane's shoulder and steering her towards the sitting-room. He led her to a small armchair near the hearth and then went and arranged for Palma to bring some drinks through.

Jane bit her lip, mortified. She had embarrassed Guy, and that wasn't in the rules. The perfect hostess didn't ever try to make her guests feel small.

In the sitting-room Ella, unperturbed, walked directly to the centre of the big, white couch, sat down and crossed one unnaturally long leg over the other, hitching her slim, elegant skirt a little in the process. Then she turned her attention to the mountain scene over the hearth. 'What is it with all these paintings? I thought you collected engineering plants—not fine art, Guy?'

Guy straddled the fat arm of the couch, his grey drill trousers tautening across his muscular thighs. Jane stole a longing glance across the room at him. Why had he had to bring that woman here? This was their special place... this was where they made love, and played man

and wife together. This was where he was learning to
respect her and would one day fall in love with her. Jane
resented intruders. Especially intruders like Ella.

'Oh, that hardly counts as fine art. It was painted by
a friend of mine, as it happens.'

'Really? Then I'm very impressed by the company you
keep, Guy. I wish I had friends who could paint that
well. It's a great picture.' She narrowed her clear blue
eyes and scrutinised it carefully... 'Kind of mean and
moody. Yeah... I can see why *you* liked it.'

'Oh, I like it well enough. But not because it's mean
and moody. It's a view of the Pennines—and very similar
to the one I could see from my bedroom window as a
child, which is why I have a special affection for it.'

'So you're a mountain boy, huh? Were your folks
farmers or what?'

Guy laughed benignly. 'Hardly. I was raised in a village
a few miles outside the city of Sunderland. But it wasn't
a thatched cottage sort of place, you know. Relatively
few of the inhabitants of that county make their living
from the land these days. My bit of England is part of
the old industrial heartland. That's my background.'

'But you *did* live in the country?'

'Oh, yes. Or at least, I spent the first eight years of
my life in a small village. Then I went to boarding-school
in Yorkshire for a few years.'

Jane sipped at her iced drink with apparent com-
posure. However, what she really felt like doing was
throwing herself off her chair and drumming her heels
on the floor. The countryside? Boarding-school?
Yorkshire? She hadn't known *any* of that.

'Eight years old? Wasn't that kind of young to go away
to school?'

Guy shrugged. 'I wanted to go. I was invited to become
a pupil at a cricket-mad prep. school by the cricket-mad
headmaster. He spotted me knocking a ball about with

a few of my pals when he was on a walking holiday, and decided he *had* to have me for the school team.'

A cricketer? She'd thought he'd had a paper-round or something...

'Guy! You mean to tell me you were one of those cute little English schoolboys? Oh, but that's just *dreamy*!' Ella gave Guy an appraising look. 'And *very* hard to believe when I look at you now. Cute you may be. But little you are not.'

Jane made herself look at Ella looking admiringly at Guy, and then she turned her eyes away and swallowed very, very hard. She had never felt more humiliated in all her life. It wasn't that Ella was flirting with Guy right under her nose—though that was bad enough. It was the fact that Ella was asking all these questions and Guy was answering them as if it were the most natural thing in the world.

She'd been married to him for two months and she didn't know any of this stuff. All he'd told *her* about his childhood was the story of the damned underground railway. She suppressed a bitter little sigh. Oh, it was all her own stupid fault, because he'd actually wanted her to ask and she wouldn't. But that was only because she'd thought it had been a painful, loveless and impoverished time for him. She had thought it would hurt him to talk about it. And she had thought that once he knew what true love really meant he would want to confide in her and she would have consoled him and promised to make it all right for him for always. This horrible woman was spoiling it all.

Guy was smiling very broadly now. 'Oh, I loved cricket so I was delighted. We even went on tour—Australia one year, and Pakistan another—to play schools over there, and then we invited West Indian and New Zealand teams to Yorkshire and arranged mini test matches over here. Admittedly it was very hard work—the team

members had to practise for three hours a day on top
of all the other school activities, so we learned self-
discipline and the value of hard work when we were very
young. But the school was great fun and I loved it. To
be honest, the person I think was hit hardest by it all
was my father. He was a very loving man, and we were
particularly close as my mother had died early on. He
got stuck into his hobbies during term-time, but he was
as excited as a puppy whenever I came home. The worst
of it was, these cricket tours were at Christmas and Easter
so I didn't get home for the traditional family holidays.
It didn't bother me one bit, but it was quite a sacrifice
for Dad. In fact, after a couple of years, he decided that
we'd have our own Christmas at a time when I could be
home with him.'

Ella gave him a sweetly sympathetic smile. 'You must
really have worked hard, you poor thing. I hope they
paid all your expenses?'

'I did have a scholarship, but my father still had to
find some fairly hefty fees to keep me there. Luckily, he
was very highly skilled at an exceptionally specialised
trade, so he could just about manage it. Later, when I
was twelve, I was offered scholarships by a number of
top public schools. But I opted to go back into the main-
stream then and live with my father.'

'So you missed out on your education?'

'Oh, no. Far from it. I had an excellent education at
the local school, and went on to study at the London
School of Economics.'

'Wow! That's a good college. Even I've heard of it.
It's kind of like Harvard Business School, isn't it?'

'Well—er—not exactly. But anyway, as it turned out,
I didn't stay there for long. I was halfway through my
degree when my father was made redundant. I was
appalled at the waste of his skills. So I raised the money

and bought up the business and put him back to work. The rest, as they say, is history.'

'You just raised the money? Like that?' She snapped her long fingers, making a practised cracking sound.

Guy laughed roundly. 'Yes. The arrogance of youth, I suppose. When I look back on it my blood runs cold. But I just walked into a branch of a high street bank and demanded a loan. It seemed very clear-cut to me, then. I loved my father, and I was going to put things right for him. The manager must have had suicidal tendencies... that's the only explanation I can think of now for his lending me so much. It was a very foolhardy thing for him to have done.'

Spoiled it all? Ella hadn't spoiled it all because there was nothing to spoil. Jane had been barking up the wrong tree from the very beginning. What a *fool* she had been. Disappointment? Rejection? Frustration? These hadn't been the driving forces in Guy's life at all. It had all been done for *love*. Which meant that he was quite capable of loving a woman. No problem there. But he hadn't gone looking for love, had he? Instead he'd gone looking for a wife. And he'd quite deliberately chosen for his wife a woman he didn't love. An illusion. Clever, huh?

'Oh, you're just too modest, Guy. You were so obviously a gilt-edged investment. There was no risk—and didn't that bank manager just know it...'

She turned to Jane. 'This gorgeous husband of yours just reeks of success, doesn't he? Anyone can tell he's the kind of man who always gets what he wants. Not the kind who would ever settle for anything but the best.'

Jane's smile nearly cracked her face in two. 'You're so right Ella. Absolutely. Guy has the highest standards in everything. But that doesn't mean you can second guess him, you know? He judges things entirely according to their purpose. So unless you know what he thinks the function of something—or somebody—should be, you've no way of knowing which choice he's likely to make. Now isn't that right, Guy?'

Guy frowned at her. She wasn't playing by the rules and he didn't like it. Her purpose as a wife was to be a charming hostess to his guests and a potential incubator for his children. Swallowing her bile, she slipped on one of her toothpaste smiles and said, 'Now, Ella, why don't I take you upstairs and show you your room and you can take a shower and then perhaps have a dip in the pool before lunch. I have a swimsuit here you can borrow if you like?'

But, naturally, Ella had the sexiest bikini in the world stowed away in her luggage. Even Jane couldn't keep her eyes off the woman's curves, wondering how they were going to be held in place by those shreds of gold string when she dived into the water. Goodness only knew what the spectacle was doing to Guy. He was wearing sunglasses as it happened, so she couldn't even begin to guess—even if his eyes had given anything away, which they surely wouldn't have done. Was he, for instance, applying his famous standards to the question of Ella's body? Was he judging it to be functionally perfect for a mistress? Ella was a career woman—not the appropriate type to make him a good wife. But, by golly, they could have a lot of fun in bed . . .

All that evening Ella displayed her evident admiration for Guy, along with her curves which she had poured into a zany little lycra number for dinner. Being in love with a man, Jane had discovered, made one acutely sensitive to his moods. She knew beyond a shadow of a doubt, for instance, that Guy was uneasy. Deception seemed to hang in the air like a premonition of thunder.

When Jane asked Ella what branch of law she specialised in, Ella was evasive.

'Oh . . . this and that. I'm a jack of all trades.'

'But surely you must favour business law or contracts or corporations or something?'

'Oh. Sure. Among other things. Yeah. Contracts, I guess.'

How odd. Because if Guy had wanted a good lawyer for a particular job, then surely he would have engaged a specialist lawyer? Not a jack of all trades. But if, on the other hand, he wanted a good lawyer for some other purpose entirely... ah, well then, a lawyer with blonde hair, luscious curves and a good line in flattering remarks might be just the ticket.

'What exactly are you and Guy working on at present?' she asked sweetly.

But lo and behold, Guy noticed a shooting star at that moment, and hurried Jane off to see it. As far as Jane could see, everything in the heavens was completely static. The universe stretched out to infinity, black, starry and cold. Not a shooting star to wish upon in sight. She shivered. For the rest of the evening she smiled a lot and gave nothing away. She really was a perfect hostess.

That night Jane made love to Guy as if her life depended on it.

The next day Ella loafed down to breakfast very late, wearing a snazzy little sun-suit. 'Oh, it's just fantastic to be able to sleep late for once! Don't you relish that, Guy? I mean, you're like me... you work long hours most of the time...'

'Mmm. It's nice to be able to sleep in. Now and again.'

'Lucky Jane. She can do it every day if she wants. She has nothing to do at all.'

'Aren't I fortunate?' Jane gloated fraudulently.

'You sure are. I just love the challenge of my career. But I do like to laze in the sun, too.'

'You've certainly got a wonderful tan,' Jane smiled.

'Huh! Now just listen to who's talking! I mean, you've got the most gorgeous tan all year round—and you don't have to work on it—nor put dollops of sun-block on your nose to stop it peeling. You are incredibly lucky.'

Jane tugged on the gold ring in her ear. 'I am,' she agreed mildly. 'I have skin like *café au lait*. The caffeine content merely increases and decreases according to the season of the year.'

'Seriously though, Jane, I'd just love to have your colouring. Just where on this earth did you get it?'

'Rio, actually.'

'Rio? Oh, fantastic. It has to be the most beautiful city in all the world. Don't you miss it?'

'I left when I was ten months old, as it happens. I don't even remember it.'

'Ah . . . I guess that explains your English accent . . .'

As Jane found herself explaining the details of her adoption she unexpectedly warmed to Ella a little. The other woman, just as Guy had been, was refreshingly open in her curiosity. Jane found it deeply flattering. Oddly enough, as Jane's manner eased with Ella, Guy's air of unease deepened. He fidgeted with his napkin, and left *The Times* crossword half-done. Eventually he went off to the diving pool. And it wasn't long after that that Ella suddenly lost interest in Jane's obscure origins, and—surprise, surprise—decided that she just *had* to work on her back somersault.

Jane watched her go with her heart in her mouth, but resisted the temptation to follow. If Guy was planning an affair with Ella, he'd presumably do it in New York. She couldn't imagine him running the risk of being caught playing footsie in his own back yard. Anyway, she couldn't stop him, and wasn't at all sure that she had any right to. Mistresses, she suspected, might turn out to be another of the rules she had failed to take into account when she let herself in for this marriage. She swam ten lengths of the pool all by herself. Very fast.

Disappointment. Rejection. Frustration. It may not be doing much for her understanding of Guy, but it was improving her breaststroke no end.

The following day Ella and Guy returned to New York. When they had gone Jane took a chair into the hall and sat in front of the Pissarro, nibbling at her thumb. She felt wasted and cold. She no longer had any hopes of making Guy fall in love with her. But she was damned if she'd let Ella breeze off with him all the same. Perhaps she *should* go ahead and try for a baby, after all... Her insides jumped with excitement at the prospect of carrying Guy's child. But her mind looked reprovingly at the idea and flinched. Babies should be conceived out of love. Two-way love. Shouldn't they?

Of course, she herself might well have been conceived without a scrap of love being involved... but that was different. She had been meant to be. The indifferent universe had mustered a little magic at the moment that she herself had been conceived. She could hardly choose to bear a child in the hope that the magic would come later, especially as she knew now that it never would. But the idea plagued her none the less for the three days that Guy was away. She had agreed to this marriage. Wasn't it her duty to have a child for Guy? Wasn't that part of the system, too...? Like mistresses...?

When Guy came back she asked, 'Guy, what if I turn out to be infertile when the time comes?'

'Are you worrying about that?'

'Not exactly. I just wondered how you'd feel. Probably because of my parents' experience, you know.'

Guy studied her from across the room. 'Is there any reason why you should think you might be?'

'No-o...'

'Then why concern yourself with a problem which may never arise?'

She shrugged, and let her eyes drop to the magazine on her lap. She was concerned because as far as she could tell an incubator which failed to incubate wasn't suitable for any purpose at all. If one married for love alone, as her mother had, then when the desired event failed to materialise, it wasn't the end of the world. But what use would Jane be as a wife if her womb didn't work?

'Jane?'

'Would you divorce me, Guy?' she asked abruptly looking up into his slaty eyes.

'Divorce you? Jane, we've only been married for a couple of months. Aren't you happy?'

'I meant if I turned out to be infertile.'

'What sort of damn fool question is that?'

'A perfectly legitimate one as far as I can see. Ours is a marriage of convenience. One of those conveniences as far as you are concerned is the begetting of children. Well, what if I'm no good at it? What then?'

'Shall we cross that bridge if and when we ever come to it?'

'Why wait to sort it out till then? Surely it can all be calculated in advance? I mean as far as I can see there are a variety of options. You could divorce me and find someone fertile to take my place. Or you could perhaps take a mistress, and have a child by her and then get custody of it and get me to adopt it——'

'What?' He sounded utterly incredulous. 'Is that supposed to be a rational option?'

Jane ignored him, merely hurrying on, 'Well, I don't see why not. After all, if it turned out that you weren't capable of fathering a child you might well expect me to have artificial insemination as a solution. Surely what I'm suggesting is no more than a sort of reversal of that process——'

'Stop it, Jane. Stop talking like this.' For the first time ever she had made Guy's iron control slip. He was really

angry. It flashed like steel across his eyes. He clearly
didn't like the idea that his wife might not be fitted to
the purpose for which she was intended.

She was frightened. But glad too. Oh, she had irritated
him time without number. And he had disapproved of
her. But those were bland, cerebral responses compared
to this fury. Wrath came from the heart. She might not
have managed to capture his heart, but she couldn't help
relishing the power she had suddenly found to stir it a
little.

'Why?' she continued rashly. 'I thought you liked
straight talking, Guy?'

'I'm not sure that this conversation is the least bit
straight. It's about as convoluted a discourse as I've ever
come across,' he muttered thunderously.

'But Guy, it's all perfectly straightforward. I can't imagine why we didn't sort all these details out before we
got married. I suppose if you'd told me that you wanted
to start a family right away I might have got round to
thinking about these things a little earlier, but——'

Guy paced across to her and grasped her wrist tightly.
Then he hauled her to her feet and looked down into
her eyes very intently. Now she understood exactly why
he normally controlled his features so carefully. This
was not the passionless man she had thought she was
marrying. He could be read like a book when he was
overtaken by emotion.

'Listen,' he growled, 'listen to me. Now that we are
married we will face these sorts of problems together,
like any other married couple. How can I possibly know
what solution will be most appropriate when the problem
itself is entirely hypothetical? For better for worse...
remember? We stood up in church and we made our
promises in front of a great many people. If getting you
pregnant turns out to be one of the ''for worses'' then

we'll look for the best solution for both of us. But I won't just dump you flat, you know. I am a man of my word, and you'd better know that.'

For better for worse...*forsaking all others*... 'Do your scruples apply to all the marriage vows, Guy?' she asked nervously.

There was a dark, ominous silence and then he said, 'No. Not all of them, Jane. You're right—our arrangement does leave loopholes after all.'

Suddenly the anger drained away from him and he let go of her wrist. He pulled her against him and held her carefully. 'What the hell has stirred all this up?'

Jane took a deep breath. She stood stiffly in the circle of his arms, fighting the temptation to lean against him and cry her eyes out. 'Solitude,' she lied wearily. 'I'm not used to living in such an isolated place—especially in a country where I don't speak the language.' It was only a white lie, anyway. Now that she knew that Guy would never fall in love with her, there was no point in staying here in this special place of theirs. Especially as it gave the Ellas of this world *carte blanche* to smarm all over her husband. 'I'm fed up here, Guy,' she continued. 'Can't we go somewhere nice together?'

They went to Genoa and boarded his yacht. Jane was charmed by the wonderful vistas of blue, blue sea glimpsed between the gorgeous white buildings of the lovely old city. Much more charmed than she was by the yacht itself, as it happened, which, though it looked absolutely splendid from a distance, with its impressive white hull and clean lines, turned out to be too ship-shape for comfort. Their state-room had been recently refitted to the highest standards, Which meant that the carpet had pile so thick you almost needed snow-shoes to walk on it, and the swagged four-poster was wide enough for six. It wasn't exactly that she had been expecting to share a hammock with Guy—though the

idea did have a lot to recommend it—but it might have
been fun to rough it just a *little*. She found herself actually willing the weather to turn. But the sun continued
to shine down on the blue, blue sea all the way to
Monaco.

Guy took her to the casino and gave her a baffling
array of chips. Jane dragged Guy off to the card tables,
begging him for instructions and advice. After a while
it began to dawn on her that she had more chips than
she'd started out with.

'You're very good at judging this,' Guy acknowledged
drily.

Jane smiled with glee and turned back to the tables.
When she had a largish pile of chips in front of her she
announced that she was bored, and cashed them in.

'Beginner's luck,' Guy smiled.

'Yes,' agreed Jane, but privately she thought that it
was more than luck. Her luck, after all, could have
turned at any moment. The important thing was that
she'd had the good sense to get out while she was ahead.

Tangled with him beneath the awning of the four
poster, she closed her eyes and let herself feel the gentle
lapping of the sea. Guy's thumb idly traced the outline
of one of her hard, dark nipples, bringing it to a state
of prickling arousal. She looked up at his face. There,
beneath his cheekbone, was that mole. The mole which
made him seem so very beautiful. She raised her own
hand and covered it, pretending to stroke his cheek as
she did so. She mustn't love him any more if she was to
survive all this. Falling out of love would be her way of
staying ahead of the game. This marriage would be so
much more tolerable if only she could manage not to
love him. But within seconds her hand had fallen away,
and all her calculations were crumbling as desire swelled
inside her and she broke, like a wave, in his arms.

They decided to live in London. Jane was relieved. It
would be easier to distract herself on home territory. In
the meantime Jane spent a few weeks travelling with Guy
while he visited his numerous plants around the globe.

'Are you sure you want to come?' he frowned. 'I don't
think you'll find it very exciting. None of these work-
shops is in very glamorous places.'

'I do want to come.'

'But why?' The yacht at the time was berthed at Cap
Ferrat, where Guy had met up with a party of acquaint-
ances who were renting a palatial house and eating and
drinking like hogs. 'You could stay here. Marcus and
Jules will look after you. You could have a lot of fun.'

Jane smiled a small smile. 'Oh, but I'll have fun travelling with you, too, Guy. Won't I?' she said.

Guy shook his head and his mouth made that straight,
disapproving line she knew only too well. But she stuck
to her guns. She was still far too much in love with him
to be prepared to leave him to his own devices.

It was an arduous three weeks. They flew to nine different locations and stayed in nine different grand hotels.
During the day Guy took small planes or helicopters or
jeeps and set off to visit his plants, which always seemed
to be located an inconvenient distance away from the
hotels. When he returned he often looked sweaty and
dusty and tired. Then he would shower and shave and
take her out to eat and then make love with her in the
hotel bed. But their lovemaking, though still ecstatic,
was conducted at a harder and faster pace than for-
merly, and afterwards Guy would fall into a heavy sleep.

'Couldn't we stay somewhere nearer?' Jane asked
plaintively at the fifth stop. 'You're away for such
ages . . . I get tired of sightseeing on my own.'

'No,' returned Guy curtly. 'There's nowhere suitable
any nearer.'

'Why are all your plants in such out-of-the-way places?' she sighed, hating to see him looking so tired, and missing the long drawn out nights of passion they had enjoyed in Tuscany.

'Look, you've got the whole of Singapore to explore. I've arranged for Annabel Roehampton to take you somewhere nice for lunch, and we're staying at Raffles, which has to be the ultimate. Isn't that enough?'

'Yes,' she murmured meekly and looked away, because her dark eyes were sharp and shiny with tears. She didn't want to have lunch with the honourable Annabel. She wanted to cook lunch for Guy, and eat it with him, preferably in bed. Their own bed.

It was quite a relief when they arrived at Heathrow. She had imagined that they would be staying in a hotel until they found a home—Guy had said very firmly that his bachelor flat wasn't suitable—but a taxi took them to central London and deposited them outside the foyer of a block of sumptuous apartments. The porter didn't know which of them to smarm over first.

'Is this really ours?' asked Jane as she was led into a fabulous drawing-room, overlooking Regent's Park, which, although furnished in Victorian style miraculously avoided looking either cluttered or dark.

'Yes. I arranged the purchase through an agent while we were away. Do you like it?'

'Did it come complete with furniture? Or did the previous people just leave everything behind?' she queried, picking up a Venetian glass paperweight from a small, walnut escritoire and examining it.

'No. I got decorators in,' said Guy, punching open one door after another and cursorily examining the rooms behind.

Jane followed him into the master bedroom. The bed was low and wide, carved from ebony, with little rails around the sides and crystal globes on each of the posts.

There were low matching tables on either side, complete with stark Japanese lamps, each bearing a calf-bound book. Puzzled, she wandered over to the bed and picked up one of the books. 'What's this doing here?' she asked.

Guy shrugged. 'Oh, just one of those touches that designers employ,' he said casually. 'I expect they put it there to make the place look lived-in.'

'So we don't even have to do our own living any more?' she snapped bitterly, discovering that the book, through beautifully bound, was in German. 'Do the designers also arrange for someone to come in and eat for us?'

Guy frowned wearily in her direction. 'What's the matter now, Jane?' he sighed.

'Nothing,' she said, and honestly, she really did try to say it in a nice voice, but her mouth twisted and her nose wrinkled and her chin puckered and she sniffed very loudly.

Guy came over to her and patted her absently on the shoulder. 'Don't you like the way they've done it? Never mind. You can get them back and have it redone any way you choose.'

And then Jane managed to straighten out her features and smile rather faintly, and say, 'No. No. It's fine. Honestly.'

Guy had sauntered back into the drawing-room, where he found a bottle of Scotch and opened it. 'It'll do for the time being,' he said, pouring himself a large measure, and then mixing a gin and orange for Jane. 'We'll have to find somewhere different when we get around to having a family. But this is perfect for the time being. It's very central.'

'Yes,' sighed Jane and took the glass from him. Then they sat on silk-covered chairs on either side of a beautiful fireplace filled with dried flowers, and sipped in unison. If anyone had come in they would have thought they looked the picture of the perfect married couple. And they were, weren't they? This was what they had married for, after all. To create the illusion of perfection. What more could a girl ask?

Autumn in London was wet and blustery. A yellow machine came past the apartment every morning, scrubbing the street. Men with bins on wheels shovelled up the leaves. A chauffeur brought a car right to the door every time she wanted to go anywhere. Jane would think of the pale, dusty road in Tuscany, turning to mud in the rain, and the diving pool, cold and abandoned and filling up with leaves. And then, of course, she would cry.

CHAPTER TEN

JANE and Guy went to dinner with her parents the week after they arrived in London. Her parents were so funny and warm and nice that she could hardly bear to be with them. They made Guy laugh for a start, which she couldn't do, and her father had a big argument with Guy over the future of genetically engineered lubricants during which Guy didn't once bother to control his features. He looked animated and cheerful, and very much alive. On top of that, her mother's apple pie went down a treat.

Jane told her mother all about the house in Tuscany and the splendid parties and the yacht and gambling in Monte Carlo, and managed to make her mother laugh lots of times without any difficulty at all. When Guy thanked her mother for the hospitality, her mother flushed with pleasure and thanked Guy in return for making her daughter so happy.

Then Wendy snuggled into the crook of Sidney's arm and said confidingly to him, 'You see, Sidney. Guy *has* made a rich man of you, after all,' and she winked conspiratorially at Jane.

'What did your mother mean by that?' Guy asked when they were back in the car.

Jane winced. 'Oh,' she said awkwardly. 'It was just a little private joke...' Naturally, believing that Jane and Guy would have no secrets from each other—that every little nuance of their history would have been picked over and cherished—her mother had seen no reason for not referring to her daughter's teasing remark.

'But what *was* the joke? That was what I meant...'

There didn't seem to be any point in lying. And anyway, it had all been harmless enough. 'Oh, it was just something that I said when Dad was in the doldrums. He thought you might ease him out of his job if ever you took over the firm, though he said you'd probably make a rich man of him in the process. Mum and I teased him, you know...'

From the silence in the car she gathered that Guy did not know.

'Um...we just said that even if *his* life was ruined, he should be jolly glad that Mum and I were going to be rich. That was all,' she finished awkwardly.

The silence persisted.

'Look, Guy, it was only a joke!' she burst out. 'You know my mother now. She wouldn't have said something like that seriously, now would she?'

'No,' conceded Guy. 'She wouldn't have.' And that was that.

A few miles further on he said, 'You must invite your parents to stay with us. You're obviously very close to them, and I like them enormously, too.'

'Yes,' said Jane. 'Perhaps they could come to lunch one Sunday. It's only a couple of hours on the motorway.'

Guy frowned. 'But Sunday is Gwen's day off, and anyway, wouldn't you like them to stay for a few days?'

Jane smiled bleakly. Not really, she thought. I don't want them examining the nuts and bolts of our relationship too closely. What she said was, 'You'd never get Dad away from Garston's for more than a day. Perhaps I'll invite Mum down when you're away on business.'

'Do that by all means. It would be an excellent idea. But it would also be nice if they both came to stay when

I was there, too,' returned Guy emphatically. 'I'd enjoy picking your father's brains, for a start. He's a bit of a genius on the quiet.'

'Is he? I'd never thought of him like that,' said Jane with surprise.

'Oh, yes. Some time ago I tried to poach a couple of his research team. They both pointed out to me that your father was the brains behind the outfit, and I'd be wasting my fat salary cheques if I employed them without also employing the creative genius behind all their new developments.'

'Oh,' Jane murmured falteringly. So that was why he had wanted to get his hands on Garston's? Thank goodness he'd given her the shares. Nobody could bid for her father's brains ever again—even Guy. 'And Dad, of course, can't be bought so easily, either,' she added cuttingly.

Guy flashed her a disapproving look. 'Your father is interested in making the perfect engine, not in making money. He's a man of great integrity, Jane. He works on projects he believes in, in circumstances he feels are right. Did you know that he'd turned down some unbelievably lucrative weapons contracts, because he didn't like the purpose for which his developments would be used?'

Jane shrugged. 'It doesn't surprise me one bit. Lining his own pockets has never been one of his priorities.'

'I've got a few ideas up my sleeve that I'm hoping will interest him,' Guy said. 'And if he goes along with me, he'll make a lot of money whether he likes it or not.'

So that was it? An extra bonus in selecting Jane for his wife was the fact that Sidney Garston's brains were there for the picking. Her father would hardly turn down his own son-in-law's contracts, now would he? A great wave of bitterness assailed Jane. One of the reasons she'd married him—oh, all right, not the real reason, which was that she'd fallen in love with him—but a reason none the less—was that she believed that by doing so she'd save her father from losing his independence to Guy Rexford. And yet it seemed she'd just sold her poor father into slavery after all. No wonder Guy had gone to so much trouble to win her parents' approval when they'd been going through their fraudulent courtship.

Jane tugged so hard on the diamond stud in her left earlobe that she almost cried out with pain. 'I can't see why you should think that that would interest me,' she muttered sourly. 'From now on I don't want to hear another word about my father and his firm.'

Guy sighed his insulting sigh. 'No, Jane. I can quite well see that it doesn't interest you. I won't bore you by talking about it further.'

And then silence really did descend. It was the sort of silence you could cut with a knife. Jane didn't dare puncture it with so much as a single word. She had seen Guy angry only once, but it was enough for her not to want to incur his wrath while he was behind the wheel of a car. Anyway, what was the point? She'd made it plain to Guy that she wasn't going to help him win her father's goodwill any further, and he was furious. She wasn't going to change her mind, so what was the point of talking?

During the evening they both made rather awkward attempts to ease the atmosphere a bit. When they went to bed, Jane wondered whether Guy might turn away from her and just go to sleep. It had never yet happened, not even when Guy had been exhausted from visiting his factories, or jet-lagged as he had been once or twice when he returned to Tuscany. But to her surprise Guy claimed her that night with an unusual tenderness. He kissed every inch of her golden, slender body. He lapped at her breasts and trailed his fingers erotically along the fine skin of her inner thighs. He kissed her knees and her toes before finally burying his freshly shaven chin in the hollows of her neck and taking her with a slow gentleness that almost had her screaming with passion.

When they at last lay spent upon the sheets she looked up at his unyielding face. Even with his eyes closed, even satiated and drained by lovemaking, his features gave nothing away.

She put one fingertip on the mole on the side of his face and said softly, 'Guy?'

'Yes?'

'Do you think we could change sides of the bed? I'd rather sleep on the right, I think.'

'Uh-huh . . .' and Guy obliging rolled over to her side of the bed, leaving her to clamber across him to the right-hand side. Now when she lay and looked at him she couldn't see the mole. Good. She didn't want to see it. She didn't want to be reminded of the extent of her own foolishness.

The next day they were back to normal. Guy dressed for work in his charcoal suit, and Jane wafted around in silk lingerie, waiting for Gwen to put their breakfast on the table.

'What are you doing today?' he said as he picked up his briefcase on the way out.

'I'll arrange some flowers this morning,' she said. 'Then perhaps I'll telephone a few friends.'

'Don't wear yourself out,' he returned, and he honestly didn't sound sarcastic. 'There's that reception tonight. Remember?'

Yes. She remembered. They'd only been in London for a week and already her social diary was filling up. Balls, receptions, dinners, parties. She would have to be very careful not to wear herself out, wouldn't she? What was more, as she pointed out to Guy, it would be awfully difficult to arrange for both of her parents to come and stay. There just wasn't the time, was there?

She and Guy took the London scene by storm. They got their photographs in society magazines and gossip columns with a frequency that was astonishing. 'Love's Young Dream', one headline read. It made Jane shed bitter tears. Because, no matter which side of the bed she slept on, there was still a surfeit of love. But the dream had quite disappeared.

Her mother came down often when Guy was abroad. Jane put on a brave face, and thought she was doing quite well. But one day her mother went out for a stroll and came back with two pounds of plums in a rustly polythene bag.

'They won't be the same as the ones off our tree,' she said, opening the bag and showing them to her daughter. 'But they'll make a nice plum duff, all the same.'

'They certainly won't be the same as the ones off your tree,' muttered Jane humorously. 'They won't be sour and hard, and there'll be an awful lot more of them in the plum duff than there usually are.'

And then her mother's blue eyes caught Jane's brown ones and they burst into gales of laughter, and, oh, no...no...it couldn't be happening, could it?... *Please* don't let it happen . . . But it *was* happening and she was helpless to stop it. Tears started to flood down Jane's cheeks and her mother's arms came around her and before she knew what had come over her, the plums were all over the Chinese rug and Jane was sobbing her heart out.

Her mother led her to the sofa and helped her sit down. She waited patiently, her arm around her daughter's shoulders until the sobs at last subsided into hiccups.

'I'm sorry, Mum...' she said, rubbing her fingertips across her damp cheeks. 'I didn't mean to do that. It's just...just...'

'Don't say anything,' her mother intruded kindly. 'You don't have to explain to me, of all people. There was only one thing in my life that ever made me cry like that, so I *do* understand. What is it? Doesn't he want children for a while? Or are you disappointed you're not pregnant yet?'

Jane covered her eyes with her hands for a moment. She couldn't possibly tell her mother the truth. 'That isn't exactly the problem...' she sighed, floundering. 'It's just that...well...my life seems so...so...'

'I know. Your life is very empty here in London, isn't it, darling? Guy's away so often with his work...but you know, it *does* all boil down to the same thing in the end. You were made for motherhood, Jane. And of course, being married has brought it one step nearer. You must feel as if you're just marking time now. I know that I did during those years when your father and I were trying. I couldn't seem to take a proper interest in anything. Life seemed so pointless for a while.' She took a deep breath. 'You must tackle Guy about it, sweetheart. He may think that he would prefer to wait a couple of years, but when he knows how unhappy it's making you he'll come around. He loves you so much, after all.'

Jane looked helplessly at her mother. What had she done by marrying Guy? She had cut herself off from first her father and now her mother. She had thrown away her birthright for...chemistry.

Matters weren't improved when Guy returned from his trip, either. They were getting ready to go out to a prestigious dinner and dance arranged to mark the end of a conference of industrialists when the phone rang.

Guy took the call in their bedroom where Jane was drying her hair.

'Ella!' he exclaimed, then turned his back on Jane, and began fiddling with his bow tie. 'Uh-huh. No. Yes. OK. Oh. About an hour? Yes. OK.'

When he turned back towards her he looked distinctly uneasy.

'No point in getting dressed up, Jane,' he said apologetically. 'That was Ella on the phone. She's in London. I have to see her urgently about business and it would help if she could be with me at this dinner tonight. You don't mind, do you? It'll only be this once.'

Jane felt as if the wind had been knocked out of her. 'No,' she said in a voice barely above a whisper, 'I don't mind.'

'She's only in town for the one night, you see, and a couple of the people involved in this deal will be at the function, so it really would be crazy not to——'

'It's OK, Guy,' she interrupted in a thin voice, sitting on a chair and bending to examine her toenails. Her damp hair hung in tendrils around her face. 'Honestly it is. No problem. Please don't apologise.' The wife who'd accepted an arranged marriage might not have the right to scream and rant when the mistress appeared on the scene, but none the less she couldn't bear to hear Guy justifying himself like this. It made her feel quite sick.

When he had gone she thought she might cry, but her tears once more had turned to gravel and refused to be shed. They felt heavy inside her. They made her angry in a dull, desolate kind of way. They made her feel that something must be done. If he was going to take a mistress when all the papers had exposed them to the world as Love's Young Dream, then he really had better do it very discreetly. She was getting rather used to her own, private humiliation. A public humiliation would be an entirely different matter.

The best thing, she decided, would be to turn up at the dinner, dressed to the nines, and make up a threesome with Guy and Ella. The Press would be able to make nothing of the fact that London's golden couple had a guest on board for the evening. Whereas if Guy were to be seen there with Ella on his own—well then the flash bulbs would pop and the tongues would wag for sure. And that just couldn't be borne.

She put on a beautiful, low-cut dress and then, having gift-wrapped herself very nicely, she had herself delivered to the appropriate hotel. She walked in with a deal of panache. She smiled her toothpaste smile. She bowed her elegantly coiffed and astonishingly beautiful head at the curious eyes of the other guests as she swept through the throng looking for Guy. Luckily, just as it was beginning to dawn on her that Guy and Ella weren't there, who should she bump into but William Gresham, big in plastics and everlastingly interested in golf.

If she had thought that going to the dinner would save her from humiliation, then she had been wrong, she reflected as she slipped into their apartment some time after midnight. Only by sticking like glue to her father's friend, and asking endless questions about putts and fairways and number three irons, had she managed to keep at bay the zillions of people just bursting for an opportunity to ask her where Guy might be. She'd even had to allow William Gresham to drive her home to protect her from the malicious questions of the throng. Once in the apartment she slipped into the bedroom and took off her dress and her shoes and her jewellery. When she confronted Guy she didn't want to be wearing the trappings of her humiliation.

She sauntered into the drawing-room, wrapped in a cosy towelling robe, her feet bare and her hair loose.

He was reading a report, but snapped it shut guiltily when she came in.

'Where have you been?' he asked.

'Out with a friend,' she returned blandly. 'How did this evening go?'

'Very well,' he said guardedly.

'Was it a good dinner?'

'Excellent,' he returned.

'Did you get your business done?'

'Er...yes. No problem.'

'And how was Ella?'

'Much the same. Fine.'

Then Jane turned her back on him and walked stoically into their bedroom. When Guy came to join her she shrugged him away. 'I'm tired,' she said into the pillow.

She was tired and yet not tired. She was tired of being married to a man who didn't love her and never would. She was tired of being an arranged wife, with none of the tender promises between them which should have been more potent than any marriage vow. She was tired of wrestling with the temptation to give in and have Guy's child in the hope that it would put things right. But she wasn't tired enough to fall asleep. She lay awake all night. When the grey, wintry dawn came she got up and went and made herself a coffee.

Then she went back to find Guy.

'I'm leaving you,' she said baldly.

He stared at her in disbelief.

'I'm sorry. But I can't handle this marriage of ours. I'm truly sorry, Guy, but I should never have got into it in the first place. You were honest with me about what it was going to entail so I don't blame you, but it's not enough.'

'Jane?'

'No, Guy...don't,' she choked out as he approached her, his hands reaching out to hold her. 'Don't touch me, please.'

He stood close to her and stared accusingly at her. 'Don't touch you? What the hell is going on?'

She took a few steps back. She was frightened to death that he would touch her and all her resolution would melt in the warmth of her desire. She was as frightened of his touch now as she had once been of his laughter, which had seemed to mock her with its promise of unreachable depths. Well, she wasn't frightened of his laughter any more, because she had sounded his depths now. Fathoms deep and icy cold, they repelled her to the bottom of her soul. He rarely laughed these days as it happened, but she wasn't prepared to wait for the time—presumably when she had borne him his children—when he rarely touched her, either. She was cutting loose. It had been a horrible mistake. Soon it would be over.

'You can't leave me, Jane,' he insisted, his face weary and hard. 'We're married.'

She forced herself to look steadily into his eyes. 'I know. And when I married you I honestly believed that we would be good together. But a marriage where not all of the vows are meant to be obeyed turns out not to be a marriage at all. The temptation to look elsewhere creeps in through the gaps, whether one wants it to or not. I was too impetuous. I should have taken my time—thought more carefully. I'm sorry to have to let you down, Guy, but that's the way it's got to be.'

There was a terrible silence. Guy's eyes raked back and forth across her face. At last he said harshly, 'Go to your parents' for a few days and think it over. Don't make *this* decision too hastily as well.'

She nodded, out of consideration for him more than anything. Because she knew she wouldn't change her mind. And oddly, as she drove herself up the M1 she realised that her father was safe once again. He would never sell his genius to Mr Guy Rexford now.

Her mother and father were badly shocked, but accepted her news unquestioningly. 'You'll tell us in your own good time—if you want to,' said her father with tears in his voice. 'And you're always our daughter, Jane. For ever and ever. There's always love and a home for you here.'

Jane went back to her old bedroom with the small window and the lumpy bed and the carpet which had been intended to make the room look feminine but which had ended up making it look like mutton dressed as lamb. She lay on her bed. Inside her the gravel shifted uncomfortably, making her eyes hurt and her throat ache. It was a terrible thing not to be able to cry.

After three days Guy turned up. Jane saw his car turn into the drive and abandoned her walk and fled to her bedroom, sprinting across the grass in her trainers as if the devil himself were after her.

She wouldn't come out of her room. She heard her parents talking and talking, and Guy's voice, deep and dangerously charming, and she bit the sheet and waited until he had gone.

'What did he say?' she asked when she came downstairs.

'He wants you back.'

'What did you tell him?'

'Nothing, love. You're our daughter. We like Guy, of course, but you're our daughter, Jane.'

'Yes. I know. I'm sorry.'

Her father handed her an envelope. 'He left you this.'

It was a cheque for a very large sum of money indeed. An astonishingly large sum of money. There was a note inside as well. It just said, "So that you can have your heart's desire, after all.'''

She folded and unfolded the note. She read it and put it against her upper lip and smelt it. She didn't do the same with the cheque. She just put that on her bedside table. Well, Guy hadn't been prepared to give her love—but then, he'd made that plain from the start. He'd always been generous with his money—but that had been part of the bargain too. She wanted to tear up the cheque, but she felt that it would be too great a betrayal of Guy. He was keeping his part of the bargain, after all. She couldn't throw it back in his face.

Guy didn't try to contact her again, and she was relieved not to have to see him. So it was a horrible shock to walk into a London hotel on a brief visit to town and find him leaning against the reception desk.

'Guy!'

He looked at her suspiciously. 'What do you want now?' he asked, and his words slashed across her skin so bitterly that her hands started to shake.

'Nothing. I'm staying here. I didn't know I was going to bump into you.'

'It's just a coincidence, is it?'

'Yes. As it happens it is. Why on earth should I have expected to find you here, anyway?'

'I'm living here for the present. I sold the apartment.'

'Oh. I hope the new people like the décor.'

He shrugged. 'I doubt they will. I expect they'll have it all ripped out and fresh stuff put in.'

'There was nothing permanent about that place, was there?' she agreed bleakly.

'Like us,' he said sardonically, and she looked away so that he wouldn't see the pain in her eyes.

And then, to her dismay, his hands came out and caught her by the shoulders. Oh, God, how she wanted him. Night after night her body had ached for him. Something in the way her shoulders drooped, in the defeated contours of her face, must have told him this, because he pulled her roughly to him and said, 'Come on. Let's go up to my suite...'

They didn't speak another word. Once the door was closed Guy loosened his tie and slipped off his jacket. He dropped it on the floor. Jane unbuttoned her coat. Little by little they shed every garment, standing wordlessly facing each other, eyes transfixed by the other's body. She saw his eyes flicker warm with desire when she unfastened her bra and let it fall on to the plush carpet. She heard her own breath catch in her throat as he unzipped his trousers and stepped out of them. Revealed at last, beautiful, golden, naked bodies. Bodies made the one for the other. Bodies which knew nothing of heartache or cool, rational thought. Bodies which once they had tasted the other, must be forever hungry. Jane reached out her hand. Guy took her fingers and led her to the bed.

And there they made love, silently, passionately, shudderingly. They made love not once but again and again and again, until the black of the night beyond dragged them, exhausted, into its blind heart.

In the morning when Jane woke up she almost cried out aloud. She had slept on his left side. He had slipped down the bed a little, so that he lay flat on the mattress, his feet hanging over the end of the bed. And he had not shaved before he took her, so that now his face was shadowed as dark as pirate's with a day's growth of beard.

Oh, now she could cry, all right. Now tears stung her eyes and demanded their release. She jumped out of bed

and gathered up her clothes and slipped on her coat,
ready to dash along the hotel corridor to her own room.

But Guy woke up. He stared at her.

'Where are you going?'

'Back to my own room.'

'Come back to bed.'

'No.'

'Why not?'

Because I'm about to cry. 'I've got a busy day.'

'Really?'

She had come to London to exchange contracts. She
had to be at the solicitors by nine-thirty, but it was still
only seven. Flustered, frightened of the power of her
own emotion, she rattled out, 'Er...yes. Really. Quite
an exciting day as it happens. I'm spending rather a lot
of your money today, Guy, you see. So...um...so I've
got to dash,' and she slammed the door behind her as
she fled.

By spring she had spent every penny. She had decided
to take the scathing words on the note at face value. She
couldn't have Guy, but perhaps she could use it to buy
a little of what her heart had once desired, after all. It
was not the most beautiful house in the world, but it
had a farmhousey quality and a modern secret passage
in the form of a concealed wardrobe. It would need a
great deal of work—the artificial fountain would need
filling in for a start, and all that nasty silk wallpaper
would have to go. In fact, she'd had to pay well over
the odds for the place, as it was being sold complete with
everything the previous owner had installed in an attempt to make the solid, eighteenth-century building re-
semble the Palace of Versailles.

But that was all to the good really. It meant there was
plenty to do, getting the place right. The work would

fill her life for years. Especially now that she was out of money and had to do it all herself.

The day the last pound was withdrawn from her account she felt light-hearted with relief. Perhaps now she could begin the long task of putting him behind her? The feeling lasted from eleven in the morning, when she visited the bank, till three in the afternoon when Guy's black Lotus pulled up outside her front door.

CHAPTER ELEVEN

GUY had a suitcase in his hand. He banged on the door almost viciously.

Bewildered, Jane went to the door and opened it, dragging her sweatshirt down over the gaping waistband of her jeans as she went. She'd lost weight these past months, and her clothes showed it.

'Guy,' she acknowledged dully as she opened the door.

'Jane Garston . . .' he drawled sarcastically.

'I still call myself Rexford, as it happens. Perhaps when the divorce is final——'

'Don't wait,' he cut in disparagingly. 'I have no desire to share my name with you any longer than is necessary.'

Jane closed her eyes briefly. 'What do you want, Guy?' she asked. She didn't blame him for showing his dislike so openly, but it hurt, none the less. She supposed that she had assumed that Guy would always maintain that air of civilised control where she was concerned.

He walked past her into the hall. He glanced about him for a moment, then seeing that the door to the drawing-room was open he went directly through. Her heart was thundering as she followed him in. His turning up like this so unexpectedly had unnerved her badly.

'What do you want?' she repeated more urgently.

He turned on his heel and looked at her with very disapproving eyes. 'I want to give you something,' he said. And then he opened the suitcase and held it high in the air, letting piles of crisp new banknotes, held together in bundles of elastic bands, pour out into a heap on the silk carpet.

He kicked contemptuously at the money. 'There's a million there,' he said cruelly. 'The bank assures me it's been counted. It's all yours, Jane Garston. You're a millionairess now in your own right.'

Jane glanced at the obscene heap of money and then up at Guy's coldly disgusted face.

'This is grotesque,' she breathed.

'Isn't it? That's why I wanted to do it. I felt it was absolutely your style.'

The shock of his words froze her for a moment. 'Why...?'

He moved his shoulders disdainfully. 'The bank told me you were down to your last fifty pounds a few days ago. I couldn't bear to think of you penniless, dear girl. Mainly because I had a nasty feeling that you might go and rip off your parents again. They're very nice people, Jane, and I found myself feeling sorry for them. Hopefully this will keep the wolf from the door until the divorce comes through and you can finally marry the man of your dreams.'

Jane began to shake horribly. She perched on the edge of a brocade-covered chair which was supported by a set of flimsy, ormolu legs. She felt sick. 'There's no other man. And as for my parents...' Her voice cracked and she had to swallow hard to bring it under control. 'Guy...I don't understand what you're getting at.'

He was looking at her so harshly she could hardly bear to meet his eyes. 'No other man? Oh, I doubt that poor Rupert Berrington has entirely given up hope yet. You could always get in touch with him and find out. Though I wouldn't if I were you. I seem to recall him making some very tasteless remarks about your origins that last time you saw him—you were very upset at the time, weren't you? Though you chose to foiget remarkably swiftly. But then you've alternatives to Rupert lined up, haven't you?'

'Guy...' She knotted her hands in her lap. 'It wasn't Rupert who said...um...and anyway it wasn't me that they...they...' she sighed bitterly. She still didn't want him to know what had been said about him, though why she should care about sparing his feelings when he was behaving like this, she really didn't know. 'Look, I really don't understand,' she finished more firmly.

'Don't you? I do. The day you walked out the phone must have rung a dozen times, you see...all those fair-weather friends you were so anxious to cultivate couldn't wait to let me know that you'd found yourself a new meal-ticket and were busily flaunting the fact. "Hanging on to his every word" was the expression most of them came up with if I remember correctly. Oh, and "insep-arable" was the other.'

Jane looked at him wide-eyed with shock. 'A *meal-ticket*?'

'I said a *new* meal-ticket. I may be rich, but I'm not as rich as William Gresham. Nor as old. No doubt he wasn't the least bit anxious to hear the patter of tiny feet at his time of life. That must have counted in his favour quite considerably.'

Jane's mouth gaped. The blood drained from her face so abruptly that it felt as if she could actually sense it sinking heavily through her veins; her ears buzzed and her brain hummed to a halt. She had trouble in catching her breath.

'Is that what you think of me, Guy?' she said a little unsteadily at last.

'Well, what do you expect me to think?'

'You...you said you were going to that dinner with Ella. So how you can imagine that I went there with Bill, I really don't——'

'Bill?' he bit out scornfully. 'And what do you call him in private? Billy Boy? Sweet William?'

'I've never spoken to him in private, as it happens. He's a friend of my father's. I've known him all my life.'

'Ah...so you've always known how rich he is—*and* that he's a widower? That must have made the decision very much easier when you hit a banqueting-hall full of extremely wealthy men—*and* wearing a dress that displayed your assets to full advantage, by all accounts. Rumour had it that you homed in on him with extraordinary speed.'

'Guy!' she groaned. 'You were out with Ella that night! Remember? You ditched me for your floozy! So don't you go accusing me of——'

'Floozy?' She made him laugh then. A dry, hateful, bitter laugh that frightened her to death. 'My God, Jane, is that what you chose to think? Did you really believe that I'd been carrying on with *Ella*? So that evening was tit for tat, was it?'

'No,' she persisted quietly.

'No!' he roared. 'It certainly wasn't, was it? Ella is young and attractive. William Gresham is old and fat, but very, very rich. There's no comparison to be made, is there?'

'No. Because I turned up at a dinner-dance expecting you to be there, and when you weren't I merely kept company with an old friend of the family. Whereas you lied and cheated and slunk off somewhere privately with Ella, and didn't care that I would surely have found out, and if you think I believe for one moment that there was nothing going on between the two of you then you're crazy. I saw the way you looked at each other!'

'You're just trying to justify yourself, little girl. You didn't really imagine that I was having an affair with Ella—you couldn't have! My God, Jane, if you really thought that then why the hell didn't you *say* something? You were my wife! We'd only been married a matter of months and we spent every spare moment we could in bed together. The whole scenario doesn't even make sense.'

'Guy! You'd more or less told me that our marriage left you free to take a mistress. I *couldn't* complain. I was simply keeping to my side of the bargain.'

'Bargain? You wouldn't know how to keep to a bargain if you took a degree in the subject. And as for my telling you...' He clapped his hand to his forehead. 'Where the hell would I have got the strength from for a mistress after the nights *we* spent together? Even if I'd been inclined to—which I most certainly wasn't—I do have my limits, you know—though I used to doubt that some nights with you.' He paused, his black eyebrows arched with incredulity. 'And to think that I thought our lovemaking was special! I suppose, having never had a lover with whom to compare me, you probably just thought it was par for the course at the time.' There was a contemptuous pause. 'Though you'll have learned differently by now, I don't doubt. That's why you couldn't wait for a top-up when you came to my hotel in London, isn't it?'

Jane sat in silence, blinking hard and staring at him with unfocused eyes. 'You were having an affair. Or planning it. You *said* you would...' she muttered wearily.

'Said what? Good God, I even remember telling you one day that I was a man of my word. That as far as I was concerned I would abide by every one of our marriage vows till death did us part. But you weren't listening, were you? You were trying to wriggle off the hook as regards having a baby and that was all you could think of, while I—fool that I was—was busy promising you my soul. But you were too busy conniving to listen.'

Desolation had crept into Jane's heart. She clasped her hands between her knees and sat in silence. She hadn't expected Guy to think well of her when she had reneged on their marriage pact, but she had never dreamed that he would have thought this badly of her. What reason had she ever given him?

'Good lord,' he continued angrily, 'I would never have forced you to have a child you didn't want. Didn't you know that? You had only to say no, once and for all . . . I admit I would have been disappointed, but there was no reason to try to convince me that you were infertile, or whatever it was that you were up to that day.' He shook his head. 'You're a bitch, Jane Garston. I'm well rid of you.' Then he touched the pile of money with his toe as if it were something foul. 'Use some of this to get yourself a better lawyer. The sooner we're divorced, the happier I shall be.'

But Jane wasn't really listening. 'You . . . *didn't* say you'd abide by all the marriage vows . . .' she insisted ploddingly, her mind scarcely functioning.

He peered at her as if she'd just emerged from a fog into his line of vision. His eyes were almost black with rage. 'Oh, no. So I didn't. You're right after all . . .' he muttered in bitingly sarcastic tones. 'I did let you off the "for richer for poorer" bit, didn't I? But then, it would have seemed awfully mean to have forced you to stay if I'd ever lost my money.'

It was too much. Jane slid off the chair on to her knees and picked up one of the wads of banknotes and hurled it at him with all her might. White-faced and wild, her lips disappearing into a thin, taut line she began to hurl the money at him. 'Keep it! I don't know what you brought it here for anyway, but it's the last thing in the world I want.'

He didn't flinch. He just stood like granite while the money bounced off him and dropped once again to the floor.

'Why don't you want it? You got through the last lot quickly enough, after all. In fact, it was discovering how quickly you'd ripped through the cash which really opened my eyes at last. Until then I thought...oh, well, it scarcely matters what I was fool enough to think now. If you don't want the money it can only mean that you've already fixed yourself up with Bill. Or is it Rupert? I keep forgetting.'

'What the hell has Rupert got to do with any of this?' shrieked Jane, confused and humiliated, and scarcely knowing what she was saying.

'He was your first target, wasn't he? And of course, it would have suited the Berringtons down to the ground. No wonder those wretched twins were so nasty when they found out you were seeing me. I feel really sorry for that young man. But at least he's been spared the horror of being married to you.'

'You're *crazy*! Certainly Rupert and I went around together for a time—but marriage was never even a possibility. We were just good friends, as the saying goes. Good grief...he never even laid a finger on me. Not once. We were friends—but it was never any more than that.'

Guy shrugged, as if the information was neither here nor there. 'If you'd really liked him, if you were *really* a good friend to him, you would have encouraged him to go his own way, come what may. If he'd been born into any other family in the land it wouldn't have mattered one bit that he was gay. Instead of which the poor chap must feel that he has at least to put up a show for his parents' sake. And you were more than ready to go along with it, weren't you? What was the temptation,

Jane? All that money? Or the title? Or was it perhaps
the fact that Rupert wasn't likely to force a baby on you?'

Jane put her hands over her face. 'Oh,' she whispered. 'Silly Rupert. It never even crossed my mind.'
Then she let her hands drop away and looked up at Guy.
'Though where you got the idea from that I was to have
married him . . . ?'

'His sisters let me know. Those nasty little twins are
very protective of their brother. They tried to warn me
off. I should have listened, but unfortunately I have an
antipathy to taking advice from little bitches like that.'

Jane shook her head. She was utterly bewildered by
the conversation. 'I wondered why they wanted me for
a friend . . .' she muttered, perplexed.

Guy groaned. 'Oh, I can tell you that. You're three
of a kind, aren't you?' He gave a scornful laugh. 'That
was the first thing I ever knew about you, as it happens.
That you were a friend of those Berrington girls. I saw
the three of you in Switzerland in February, you know,
chucking lumps of ice at a bunch of frozen photographers. I swore to forget you then—but I'm afraid your
face isn't quite so easily forgotten, Jane *Garston*.'

'Switzerland?'

'Yes. You know. That rather hilly country smack bang
in the middle of Europe.'

Flummoxed, Jane found herself struggling to rec-
ollect . . . 'Were you there that day?' she said heavily,
remembering at last. 'The ambulance took ages, didn't
it? That poor girl—she was in agony. And all that those
wretched Pressmen could do was to try to get close-ups
of her face. They were dreadful . . . they had those huge
telephoto lenses . . .'

A look of mystification passed over Guy's face.
'Agony?' And then he dismissed her comments. 'Look,
those photographers congregate there because the place

is full of imbeciles like you who like nothing better than to be photographed cavorting with the rich and famous. They're just doing their job—and a bloody hard job it must be when they get pelted with ice by a bunch of rich bitches just for the fun of it.' He let out a scornful laugh. 'I didn't hear you complaining about the Press when they were busy plastering your face all over the society magazines. "Love's Young Dream". Remember?' And he gave another bitter, humourless laugh.

Jane shook her head as if to rattle her thoughts into order. This was one of his horrible misapprehensions which she *had* to put right. It wouldn't be fair on that poor girl who had fallen, otherwise. 'The Berringtons took me skiing with them, Guy. I went because I like skiing, as it happens, not to get noticed. But that particular day a woman fell and broke her leg. She started to miscarry while she was lying on the snow waiting to be taken to hospital. It was awful. She was breaking her heart and feeling so dreadfully guilty because she knew it was all her own fault, and those rats from the newspapers just wanted to turn it into a good story. They didn't get their pictures, though. We made sure of that.'

She turned to Guy, her eyes bright with tears. 'You didn't keep your eyes and ears open that day, did you? Nor for all the days of our marriage. You haven't got a clue about me, Guy. You've got me wrong from start to finish. Now why don't you go away. Go back to Ella and help her with her back somersault or whatever it is you do together. But just leave me alone.'

She dragged the suitcase across the floor to where she was kneeling and began to load armfuls of money into it, tears beginning to drip off the end of her nose. 'Take this away with you now. I shall sell this house and give you the other money back as soon as I can. I only spent it because of your note. I thought I was keeping faith with you in a stupid sort of way. Now that I know exactly what you think of me this house wouldn't give me a moment's pleasure.'

'You've certainly had plenty of fun with it so far,' he jeered. 'Decorating...furnishing...gardening.'

'So the bank has been feeding you details of my cheques? I'm surprised at them. Still, it won't bother me any more. I shan't be spending any more of your rotten money, so I won't have to go near that bank ever again. Luckily there'll always be a home for me with my parents.'

Guy bent down and grasped her wrist, pulling her to her feet. She didn't mind being touched by him now. He could no longer move her. Not now.

'Oh, no. You're not going back there until I've spelled out a few home truths to you. Your parents are very exceptional people, and it's about time you understood that, instead of grouching about the fact that they weren't rich enough for your liking.'

That was when Jane hit him. She raised her arm and brought her fist crashing down against his jaw and then flew at him, fists flailing madly and even her teeth parted ready to bite. But he grabbed her by her arms and held her firmly at arm's length.

When his fingers clamped hard against her flesh she felt herself shudder with revulsion. Whether it was that, or simply a return of her plain old common sense she couldn't tell, but at any rate the fight abruptly went out of her. He was far too strong. It was pointless. She stood limply, allowing his hand to scald the fine bones of her wrist.

'Don't say that!' she protested bitterly. 'How could you? You don't know anything about me!'

He shook his head wearily. 'If I don't, then it's not for want of trying to understand you, Jane. I tore myself

to shreds trying to understand the forces that had made
you what you were. Mainly so that I could set about
changing you, I have to admit—which was a crazy thing
to do, because people never change. Not really. But at
least I *tried*, Jane, which is more than you ever did. You
never even asked me one single question! If you knew
how I yearned to tell you about myself—but you didn't
give a damn, did you?' He sighed. 'I don't suppose you
liked the fact that I was a self-made man. You couldn't
bear to think of me, in a terraced house, being brought
up by someone who soiled his hands as an engineer. You
don't even like to think of your own father working in
an engineering plant, albeit in a collar and tie, so what
you would have made of my father in his boiler suit
doesn't bear thinking about.'

Jane tried to swallow but her mouth was too dry. 'It
wasn't like that. That wasn't why I didn't want to talk
about your work.'

'Wasn't it? Right from the start you made it plain you
hated anything to do with engineering. "Horrible place"
you said when I mentioned your father's works.'

'Swarf...' she found herself saying weakly, her eyes
screwed tight. 'I hated the swarf, you see. I was
frightened—there was a nightmare—this monster with
swarf for hair—I was only a little girl, but I can't help
the fact that it's stayed with me. And on top of that, I
thought you were going to buy Garston's and you just
wanted to get information out of me. That's why I
wouldn't talk about it.' She looked bleakly into his dark
eyes. 'And...oh, if you think that I'm a snob...oh,
Guy, if you think that...that I'd...' She started to cry
properly then, great dry, racking sobs which made her
face contort and her mouth open wide like a child's.

'You didn't understand me...' she gasped at last. 'How
can you say that you tried to understand...? When you

think that all I'm interested in is money? When you think that I feel like that about Mum and Dad? How can you say that, Guy? How can you?'

He let go of her then, dropping her cruelly so that she crumpled into a heap on the floor. 'Oh, I certainly did want to understand you, Jane,' he sighed, and she sensed that he, too, was losing the spirit for this pointless, dreadful fight. His voice, at any rate, was low and expressionless, as if drained of vitality by a terrible fatigue. 'That's what I employed Ella for. That's why I brought her out to meet you. You see, I was fool enough then to believe you when you said that you wanted a baby, but there was something deep holding you back. It hadn't clicked then that you didn't want children at all and were just stalling me. I thought ... well, it occurred to me that maybe it was your background in Rio that was the trouble. So I employed Ella to try to trace your mother. Her firm specialises in that sort of thing. She's the best.'

Jane looked up at him, startled. 'You had me checked out? I knew you wanted to marry me for my social standing—oh, and maybe for my beauty too, if I'm honest with myself. But I didn't know you'd go so far as to try to ascertain that all my relatives were also perfectly respectable people with perfect bone-structure and nice hair!'

'Oh, good lord, Jane ...' Guy's face contorted with exasperation. 'Don't be so stupid! I wanted you to be the mother of my children from the moment I set eyes on you in Switzerland. I didn't know a damn thing about you then. I didn't care who you were or where you came from.'

'But you married me for my social standing, Guy! You made it very plain!'

'Married you for your...' He made a disparaging noise with his tongue and teeth. 'Where the hell did you get that idea?'

'When you asked me to marry you... that night... in the car... I asked you to spell out the reasons and——'

'You asked me to have an affair! I was spelling out the reasons why I *didn't* want an affair with you—why it had to be marriage!'

She shook her head, bewildered. 'So why,' she challenged bitterly, 'did you check me out?'

Disdain began to creep back into the weary lines of his face. 'Because I thought maybe you were frightened to have a child, knowing so little of your genetic inheritance. I thought maybe finding out would help.' He paused for a moment and then said, 'Of course, I guess I checked you out right from the start in Switzerland. But only to find out who you were and to figure out how to get to meet you. It seemed like a stroke of luck that you came from a family who were involved in engineering, too. Almost as if it were meant to be.'

A watery smile broke at the corners of his mouth and then fled. 'I could have got to know you through those dreadful Berringtons, of course. I could have wangled an invitation to one of their parties and had myself properly introduced to you and invited you to the opera. But I much preferred the option of getting to know you through a man whose reputation I already held in great esteem. Because it was the knowledge that you were Sidney Garston's daughter which foolishly led me to believe that you couldn't be as shallow as you seemed. Wishful thinking, I'm afraid.'

Jane closed her eyes. Then she put her hands over her face. 'You were trying to take over the firm,' she mumbled, her head spinning. '*That's* how you got to know me.'

'I wasn't, as it happened. Though I was naturally very interested in your father's work. I only bought the shares because you complained that you didn't own a single one. And then when I realised why it mattered to you—because your father didn't have a big enough holding to secure your inheritance, I started buying them with a view to giving them to you when I'd courted you.'

'But you *didn't* court me,' Jane said sadly, as the picture began to come clear in her mind. 'You gave up on it.'

'Yes. Well. I tried telling myself that there was no such thing as love at first sight. That's when I decided to get to know you properly. So that I could fall in love with you properly, you see, without any of this love-at-first-sight mumbo-jumbo clouding the issue. Though that plan had to be abandoned when you made it plain you didn't want to know anything about me or my background or my work or my family or my schooling, or any other damned thing that might have concerned me. And then I discovered that you were already considering marrying Rupert Berrington and I figured that the courtship ritual wasn't exactly necessary as far as you were concerned. You were already quite happy with the idea of a marriage of convenience—although you didn't like having it put so bluntly, did you? Didn't like it one bit. I was fool enough to be pleased by that. I figured I'd got you wrong...that it *could* all work after all.'

Jane twisted the stud in her ear so fast that it hurt. He had loved her from the start...? No...that wasn't right. He had only *thought* he had loved her. Because if he had really loved her, then how could he have got her so badly wrong? And by the same token she must have got her own feelings for him just as badly wrong. She had never loved him, after all. Because if she had really loved him she would never, ever have misunderstood him in the way that *she* had, would she?

Though it was odd, very odd, because she *felt* as if she loved him—even now. Looking up at his saturnine features, that unyielding mouth, the short, dark hair, and his blue-black eyes, she felt a great wail of love cry out inside her. Except that it wasn't love, because they didn't even know each other. Shakily she stumbled to her feet. 'Guy,' she sighed, not knowing where to begin, 'you just said that you loved me.'

'Yes. Well, I guess I was wrong about that.'

She nodded slowly. 'You were. All the things you've accused me of today are dreadfully, horribly wrong. Which means that you never knew me. So you couldn't have loved me.'

And then, when she looked into his eyes he looked away. But not before she saw tears standing there.

'It felt as if I knew you once or twice...' he said thickly. 'Windsurfing...I wanted to catch hold of you in the water...and then the next day, when you rubbed that sand into my back.' He stopped talking very abruptly, and redrew the lines of his face into their familiar mask. 'I was wrong,' he finished stiffly. 'I was physically obsessed by you, Jane. That was all. I wanted you so badly I could hardly control myself. Once we were engaged it was intolerable. I had to keep out of your way, because I didn't trust myself.' He let out a pained sigh. 'Though why I bothered...? Of course, I thought we were going to be married for ever then. I wanted to start it right. To earn your respect. To build us a solid foundation.'

Jane's lower lip was trembling and her eyes were so bright that she had to blink several times before she could see clearly. When she had mastered her emotions she continued staunchly, 'I'm not trying to tell you that you've got me wrong in order to save my own face, you know? If I were really the money-grubbing little bitch you seem to think that I am, then of course then I'd be bound to tell you that you'd got me wrong, because I don't suppose even money-grubbing little bitches like to admit that that's what they are. So I can't prove to you that I'm telling the truth. All I can do is to tell it.'

She took a deep breath, aware that Guy was looking resolutely at the floor, determined not to meet her eye. 'I'm telling you that you've got me wrong because I don't want you to pity my family, Guy. They're remarkable people. As you once pointed out, I'm very close to them. It was easy to let go of them when I married you... because...' Even now she couldn't bring herself to admit to him that she loved him. It would seem too pat. He would never believe her—and anyway, he didn't love her any more, so it would be too humiliating. Instead she fumbled for another version of the truth. 'Because... they aren't the clinging type. And they wanted me to marry you. They always wanted me to have what was best for me.'

'But Jane, don't you realise that what they want for you isn't wealth but happiness?' His eyes burned with intensity, and he put out a hand towards her, but didn't touch her. 'Ella didn't find out much. But she discovered that there had been a Brazilian family trying to adopt you, too. They were wealthy and already had two sons. The wife didn't want to go through another pregnancy, and anyway, she wanted to make sure that this time round she had a pretty little girl. Your mother fought tooth and nail to make sure that she got you. She didn't care whether you were pretty or not. She was frightened that this family might reject you if you turned from a beautiful baby into a plain child. Good lord, your mother even told me that she chose your name because it was nice and ordinary and you'd never feel that you had to live up to it in any way. Do you want any more proof than that that all your parents wanted for you was happiness?'

'But of course! I never had any doubt about that!'

He shook his head. 'That's not what you said on our wedding-day.' And he sighed such a grey, heavy sigh that all of the breath seemed to shake out of his body. 'When I asked you whether you'd decided that love didn't matter, after all,' he continued, 'you said you were marrying me so that your parents could see you getting everything. In abundance. Anyhow, it was quite plain what I was offering when I asked you to marry me...the sort of lifestyle you wanted to be able to afford. *That's* what you thought your parents wanted for you. *That's* why you married me.'

'It was what you offered. But that wasn't why I accepted. I...' She swallowed hard, making a heroic effort to see this through in a dignified way. He didn't love her any more, so it wouldn't hurt him that it was all over. But she didn't want him to be left with a residue of bitterness for the rest of his life. Not when it was so unnecessary. 'Guy, for all sorts of reasons I felt that fate was taking a hand and I should go along with it. I...I love my family, and I guess I'd always believed that fate had placed me with them. Fate had given me friends from other cultures along the way—friends who told me that love inside a marriage would grow from respect. I really believed when I accepted you that that would happen. I honestly thought it would work. I was wrong, of course.'

'But Jane,' Guy said in a voice thick with despair, 'how could you have hoped to come to respect me when you wouldn't even let yourself get to know me?' He paused to reflect for a moment. 'You know something? It occurred to me, when Ella came over to Tuscany, that when I was telling her about my background it was probably the first time you'd ever heard about it, too... It shook me. Because I thought by then that we were getting somewhere... I really did... though it must have been an illusion. I liked being cut off with you there, all alone. But you were hankering after parties and crowds, and I'd promised you a good social life, because that was what you wanted. But we were *better* all alone. I'm sure.'

He let out a weary sigh. Then he put up a hand to cover his eyes.

It was a gesture of such numbing vulnerability that she could barely hold herself back from rushing across to him and holding him in her arms. Only the knowledge that he would disdain her comfort held her back.

He let his hand drop and looked at the suitcase at his feet. 'I'll go.'

'Take it with you, Guy,' she said, bracing herself for his final departure.

He stuffed his clenched fists in his trouser pockets. 'Yes,' he said. But she could see that he was nowhere near as calm as he would like her to think, and scarcely fit to drive.

'Let me make you a cup of tea first,' she offered impulsively. Then added with a weak smile, 'No sugar. See? I remember.'

He nodded ruefully. 'That was about the nearest you ever got to cooking me a meal, wasn't it? I should have realised from that that it wasn't going to work. My father was great... and he did finally master the art of the Sunday roast, but I have to admit I always fantasised about having a woman to put a meal on the table for me... Oh, I know it's old-fashioned and sexist, and I knew perfectly well that you weren't going to be that sort of wife...' He gave a resigned smile. 'That's why I did the cooking myself—to make sure I didn't start getting stupid ideas... But we can't just throw away our histories, can we?' He sighed. 'I made a mess of it, Jane.

I couldn't accept you for what you were. I guess I should have stuck to engineering. I will in future.'

'No, Guy,' she said softly, leading the way into the kitchen and determined to be strong until the bitter end. 'You'll make someone a fine husband one day—and you'll be a wonderful father, some day too. But next time you make those vows, just make sure that it's with someone you really love, huh?' *And who loves you too*, she prayed inwardly.

'And what about you, Jane?' he asked, pulling out a captain's chair from the scrubbed pine table and sitting down.

Jane filled her heavy kettle and put it on the hotplate of the Aga. She couldn't bring herself to speak. Instead she just shrugged awkwardly.

'I admit I seem to have got it wrong about Rupert and that Gresham bloke. But is there anyone in your life who's likely to make you happy—without the intervention of fate, that is?'

She shook her head so that her glossy hair swung about her face. 'Nope,' she said at last, when she had forced down the surging emotion that was threatening to overwhelm her. 'I've been pouring all my affection into this house, so far, and I'm beginning to think inanimate objects are my forte, too. I haven't done all the work yet— but it shouldn't be difficult to sell, even so. I'll send you the money as soon as I can.'

He pulled a face. 'Don't be crazy. You can keep this house. Keep that bloody suitcase full of bank notes too. I don't care.'

'But I do. I don't need this place—or even want it after all the things we've said today. I can't repay you for all the damage I did when I agreed to marry you for the wrong reasons, but at least I can repay you in material terms. I'll put it on the market right away.'

He looked around at the big, farmhouse-style kitchen. 'From what little I've seen the rest seems pretty much complete. I suppose you were bound to leave the kitchen to last. There's no point in preparing all that party food until you're ready to give the house-warming party, is there?'

Jane gave a wry laugh. 'On the contrary. The kitchen's the only bit I *have* touched.'

'But all the rest is so——'

'So ghastly. I know. I don't know if I would ever have succeeded in turning this place into the home I wanted. I certainly didn't make much of a job of stripping the paint off the dresser. There are little bits left all over the place. I'm afraid it's a family failing, not getting things quite right. Never mind.' She went across to the breadbin and produced a heavy, grey-looking loaf. 'Do you want a slice? I'm afraid I haven't much else in.'

He nodded. She cut him a piece and buttered it, setting it on a plate in front of him before going to warm the pot.

He took a bite. 'I'd change my baker if I were you.'

She looked across the kitchen at him. His dark eyes met her black ones for just a moment. And then suddenly, helplessly, she burst into gales of laughter. But the laughter brought tears to her eyes. Tears of grief. She stopped herself.

'Why did you laugh?'

She started again then, almost hysterically, blinking hard while her shoulders shook convulsively. 'Oh, Guy! Your face! You look just like you must have done when you were a schoolboy,' she managed to say, desperately willing the powerhouse of emotion within her to wait until he had gone before roaring into action . . .

He frowned uncertainly, chewing on the heavy piece of bread.

She pulled herself together at last. 'I made the loaf,' she confessed with false brightness. 'You can spit it in the bin, if you like.'

He swallowed determinedly, then looked down at his slice. He pushed the plate away. 'It's horrible. What made you try?'

'It beats the hell out of stuffing olives,' she said, wishing now that she'd never offered him the cup of tea. All of a sudden they were so near to understanding one another. And yet it was all so dreadfully impossible... She reached a couple of mugs down from the dresser, and as she did so her sweatshirt rode up.

'Good grief...I can count your ribs...' muttered Guy.

'I...I've been working hard. I guess I have lost a bit of weight.'

'You haven't been dieting?' he asked, and his voice was rough with concern. It lay against her skin like swansdown. 'Because, Jane, that would just be dumb. You've got the world's most perfect figure——'

She kept her back to him. She lined up the two mugs so that their handles faced each other. She set the pink mug to the left of the blue one. 'No. I haven't been dieting.'

She raised one hand to stroke at her throat where the words still nestled tenderly. And then she slowly turned to face him, her dark eyes frightened, her face pale. 'I wouldn't do that,' she said shakily, her voice barely above a whisper. 'It can jeopardise one's fertility, so I've heard.'

He looked into her eyes, and then his features forgot everything they had ever learned during all those years of boardroom manoeuvring. They dissolved into lines of uncertainty. And in his eyes flickered the first dawning of hope...

'But that wouldn't bother you...' he said cautiously.

She gave a single nod. 'It would. I...I didn't want a nanny, Guy...but that didn't mean I didn't want a child.'

The light in his eyes brightened one degree. 'But the opera...the parties...theatre outings to Stratford...you can't do any of that with a baby in tow, you know?'

'I know,' she said simply. And then she closed her eyes tight, although it didn't stop the tears from running free. 'But I've got this wonderful recording of *Rigoletto*—though I can't listen to it too often because it makes me cry—and...and I have this book of Shakespeare's sonnets...they're far more romantic than the plays, you know? I can recite some of them off by heart, if you'd like to listen some time... And as for company...well, there's only one person's company I really want of an evening.' She gulped, and a huge sob burst out. Then, eyes still tight shut, she steeled herself to say the next bit. 'But I don't really know him. I've been waiting for him to introduce himself from the first moment I met him. I kept telling myself that there was no such thing as love at first sight. That it was only chemistry...and that I couldn't really love him because I didn't know him... But...um...um...'

And then they were there. His arms. They were around her shoulders, holding her so tight, and his mouth was in her hair and his rough chin was butting her cheek and underneath her own hands she felt the emotional surge of his ribcage match her own.

They never got round to drinking the tea. They made love so tenderly and yet so swiftly that it didn't have time to get cold. But lying upstairs in the Louis-Quinze bedroom they could neither of them bear to leave the other to go down to fetch it.

'This room is horrible,' said Guy, rubbing his mouth against her skin.

'Mmm. Don't talk about it.'

'The whole house is horrible.'

'I know. But it's got potential. I love it.'

'Has it?'

'Mmm. For a start, the windows are big.'

'Well, yes...'

'There's even a chipboard secret passage...'

Guy groaned. 'Don't talk to me about secret passages, or I shan't be able to control myself...'

And then Guy's dark blue eyes met Jane's dark brown ones and they both stared at one another for a long, long moment, while the universe, once more, mustered its magic. And then suddenly, together, for the first time, they burst into gales of laughter.

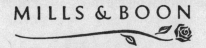

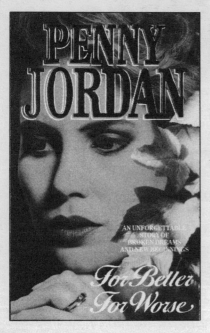

Next Month's Romances

Each month you can choose from a wide variety of romance with Mills & Boon. Below are the new titles to look out for next month, why not ask either Mills & Boon Reader Service or your Newsagent to reserve you a copy of the titles you want to buy – just tick the titles you would like and either post to Reader Service or take it to any Newsagent and ask them to order your books.

Please save me the following titles:	Please tick	✓
A MASTERFUL MAN	Lindsay Armstrong	
WAITING GAME	Diana Hamilton	
DARK FATE	Charlotte Lamb	
DEAREST MARY JANE	Betty Neels	
WEB OF DARKNESS	Helen Brooks	
DARK APOLLO	Sara Craven	
BLUE FIRE	Sarah Holland	
MASTER OF EL CORAZON	Sandra Marton	
A WAYWARD LOVE	Emma Richmond	
TANGLED DESTINIES	Sara Wood	
THE RIGHT KIND OF MAN	Jessica Hart	
DANGEROUS ENTANGLEMENT	Susanne McCarthy	
THE HEAT OF THE MOMENT	Kay Gregory	
AN EASY MAN TO LOVE	Lee Stafford	
THE BEST-MADE PLANS	Leigh Michaels	
NEW LEASE ON LOVE	Shannon Waverly	

If you would like to order these books in addition to your regular subscription from Mills & Boon Reader Service please send £1.90 per title to: Mills & Boon Reader Service, Freepost, P.O. Box 236, Croydon, Surrey, CR9 9EL, quote your Subscriber No:.................................. (if applicable) and complete the name and address details below. Alternatively, these books are available from many local Newsagents including W H Smith, J Menzies, Martins and other paperback stockists from 14 October 1994.

Name:...

Address:..

....Post Code:..........................

To Retailer: If you would like to stock M&B books please contact your regular book/magazine wholesaler for details.

You may be mailed with offers from other reputable companies as a result of this application.
If you would rather not take advantage of these opportunities please tick box. ☐